THE GUILTY RIVER

WILKIE COLLINS

THE GUILTY RIVER

ALAN SUTTON

First published 1886

First published in this edition in the United Kingdom in 1991
Alan Sutton Publishing Ltd · Phoenix Mill · Far Thrupp · Stroud
Gloucestershire.

British Library Cataloguing in Publication Data

Collins, Wilkie, *1824–1889*
    The guilty river
    I. Title
    823.8 [F]

    ISBN 0–7509–0010–5

Cover picture: Winter Days, 1888, *George Henry Boughton, courtesy of the Fine
Art Society, London. (Photograph: The Bridgeman Art Library.)*

Typeset in 9/10 Bembo.
Typesetting and origination by
Alan Sutton Publishing Limited.
Printed in Great Britain by
The Guernsey Press,
Guernsey, Channel Islands.

CONTENTS

BIOGRAPHICAL NOTE

WILLIAM WILKIE COLLINS was born on 8 January 1824, in New Cavendish Street, London, the elder son of William Collins, a fashionable and successful painter of the early nineteenth century, who counted among his friends Wordsworth and Coleridge. William Collins was a religious man, and in his strict observances may have been a repressive influence on his son, who appears to have inherited his mother Harriet Geddes's attractive and friendly personality. Wilkie was named after his godfather, Sir David Wilkie, RA, a bachelor and close friend of the family.

Little is known of Wilkie's early life. His brother, Charles, was born in 1828, and the family lived comfortably, first in Hampstead, then in Bayswater, where Wilkie attended Maida Hill Academy. The following year the whole family left for Italy, where they spent two years, visiting the major art collections and learning Italian. On their return, Wilkie attended a private boarding school in Highbury, where his storytelling talent was recognized and exploited by a senior prefect who demanded, with the threat of physical violence, to be entertained. 'Thus,' wrote Collins, 'I learnt to be amusing on a short notice and have derived benefit from those early lessons.'

When he left school in 1840, he showed no inclination to enter the Church, as his father wished, and chose, without enthusiasm, the world of commerce, accepting a post with Antrobus & Co., tea importers. He was totally unsuited to the regularity of business life, preferring to escape to the vibrant atmosphere of Paris. He started to write articles and short stories, which were accepted for publication, albeit anonymously, and in 1846 his father agreed that he should leave commerce and take up law, which would, in theory, provide him with a regular income. He studied at Lincoln's

Inn Fields, and was finally called to the bar, but his legal knowledge was to be applied creatively in his novels, rather than practically in the law courts.

In his early twenties Collins was painting as well as writing. He had many friends who were artists, and he supported the new Pre-Raphaelite movement. In 1848 he had a picture exhibited in the Royal Academy. In the same year his first book was published: the memoirs of his father, who had died the previous year. These were diligently researched and provided a training ground for the emerging writer, developing his thorough methodical approach to compilation and exercising his descriptive ability. His first novel, *Antonia* was published by Bentley two years later. Although of no great literary merit, it was written in the then popular mode of historical romance, and so enjoyed instant success. The following year Bentley published *Rambles Beyond Railways*, an account of a holiday in Cornwall, which reflected Collins' life-long love of wild and remote places.

It was in the same year, 1851, that Wilkie Collins first met Charles Dickens, an introduction effected by their mutual friend, the artist, Augustus Egg. The meeting was significant for both, leading to a close friendship and working partnership from which both benefited. Dickens had found a friend of more stable temperament than himself, affable and tolerant, responsive to his restless demanding nature. From Collins he acquired the skill of economic and taut plotting, as evidenced in *A Tale of Two Cities* (which may be interestingly compared with Collins's story of the French Revolution, *Sister Rose*, 1855), and in his later novels. Collins was welcomed by the Dickens family, and spent many holidays with them in England and France. He was encouraged and guided in his writing by Dickens, and he must have been stimulated by the latter's enthusiasm and vitality. The two authors worked together on Dickens' magazines, *Household Words*, and *All the Year Round*. Collins was employed as an editor, and many of his works appeared first in these publications, while both writers collaborated on several short stories.

A Terribly Strange Bed – Collins's first work in the macabre genre – was the first of his short stories to appear in *Household Words*, in 1852. The following year the magazine saw the publication of *Gabriel's Marriage*, a story of a Breton fishing community. In the interim, Dickens had turned down *Mad Monkton*, a study of inherited insanity, as unsuitable subject matter, and this was later published by *Fraser's Magazine* in 1855. These two, along with *Sister Rose, The Yellow Mask*, and *A Stolen Letter*, were originally published in *Household Words*, and reprinted in *After Dark*, 1855, for which anthology Collins wrote the successfully economic and melodramatic *Lady of Glenwith Grange* (an inspiration for Miss Haversham?). *A Rogue's Life*, Collins's venture into the picaresque, was serialized in 1856. This was followed in 1857 by *The Dead Secret*, a full length novel, which in its complexity suggests the author's technical potential. *The Biter Bit*, which was published in 1858 and is commonly held to be the first humorous detective story, shows Collins's development of the epistolary form. Both of his two greatest novels, *The Woman in White* and *The Moonstone*, appeared first as serializations in *All the Year Round* – as did the less well known *No Name*. This unconventional study of illegitimacy was published in its full form in 1862, two years after the masterpiece of suspense and drama *The Woman in White* and six years before his original detective story, *The Moonstone*, appeared as complete books.

Another interest shared by Collins and Dickens was a love of the theatre. *The Frozen Deep*, 1857, written by Collins and starring Dickens, was inspired by an interest in the Arctic exploration of the time. It was followed by a series of minor productions, the stage version of *No Thoroughfare* (with combined authorship), enjoying a record run of two hundred nights in 1867.

Anyone meeting Collins in those days would have seen:

> A neat figure of a cheerful plumpness, very small feet and hands, a full brown beard, a high and rounded forehead, a small nose not naturally intended to support a pair of large spectacles behind which his eyes shone with humour and friendship.

> R.C. Lehmann, *Memories of Half a Century*

But how many would have glimpsed, as did the young artist, Rudolf Lehmann, the strange far-off look in his eyes, which gave the impression of investing 'almost everything with an air of mystery and romance'? It was suggestive of a depth of personality not accessible to many, but demonstrated by the author's expressed unconventional views of the class and social *mores* of the day; which were further borne out by what is known of his personal life. During the 1860s, Collins met and fell in love with Caroline Graves, who had a daughter by a previous marriage. He never married her, but lived with mother and daughter for most of the remainder of his life. In 1868, Caroline mysteriously married another, and Collins entered into a relationship with Martha Judd, by whom he had three children. However, by the early 1870s, he was once more living with Caroline, who was still known as Mrs Graves. It has been suggested that Martha Judd may have been employed originally by Collins as an amanuensis. Over the years Collins's health had been deteriorating. He was a victim of gout, which attacked his whole body, including his eyes. He suffered a particularly severe attack in 1868, when his mother died, and he was working on *The Moonstone*. A dedicated woman, capable of disregarding his suffering and attending only to his words was employed, to whom Collins dictated the rest of the work, but she has never been named.

In 1870 Charles Dickens died. During the previous ten years Collins had produced his best work: the three novels serialized in *All the Year Round*; *Armadale*, 1866, in the *Cornhill Magazine*, and *Man and Wife*, 1870, in *Cassell's Magazine*. But with Dickens' death, something in Collins seemed to die too, although his popularity remained undiminished. His novels, produced regularly until his death, were widely read, and his was some of the first fiction to appear in cheap editions. In the 1870s he enjoyed some success with the stage versions of his novels, which were produced both in London and the provinces. Not only was Collins's work popular in England; his novels and plays were translated and produced in most European countries, including Russia, and were widely available in America. In 1873 Collins was invited to give readings in the eastern United States and Canada. Although his reading lacked the vitality of Dickens, the Americans were charmed by him.

Of course, it was not only Dickens's death which adversely affected Collins's work. His gout was becoming persistent, and he relied increasingly on laudanum to relieve the pain. However, he never lost his mental clarity, taking care to be properly informed about medicine, drugs and chemistry, as is clearly shown in *Heart and Science,* 1883 and the detailed notes he left for his last novel, *Blind Love,* 1890 – completed, posthumously, at his request, by Walter Besant. During his later years, his social life was restricted by poor health, but he did not become a recluse as has been suggested. He maintained close friendships with Charles Reade, Holman Hunt, the Beard and the Lehmann families, and theatrical people, including Ada Cavendish and Mary Anderson. In 1889, after being involved in a cab accident, Collins's health rapidly declined, and he died while suffering from bronchitis on 23 September. He was buried at Kensal Green Cemetery.

SHEILA MICHELL

CHAPTER I

ON THE WAY TO THE RIVER

For reasons of my own, I excused myself from accompanying my stepmother to a dinner-party given in our neighbourhood. In my present humour, I preferred being alone – and, as a means of getting through my idle time, I was quite content to be occupied in catching insects.

Provided with a brush and a mixture of rum and treacle, I went into Fordwitch Wood to set the snare, familiar to hunters of moths, which we call sugaring the trees.

The summer evening was hot and still; the time was between dusk and dark. After ten years of absence in foreign parts, I perceived changes in the outskirts of the wood, which warned me not to enter it too confidently when I might find a difficulty in seeing my way. Remaining among the outermost trees, I painted the trunks with my treacherous mixture – which allured the insects of the night, and stupefied them when they settled on its rank surface. The snare being set, I waited to see the intoxication of the moths.

A time passed, dull and dreary. The mysterious assemblage of trees was blacker than the blackening sky. Of millions of leaves over my head, none pleased my ear, in the airless calm, with their rustling summer song.

The first flying creatures, dimly visible by moments under the gloomy sky, were enemies whom I well knew by experience. Many a fine insect specimen have I lost, when the bats were near me in search of their evening meal.

What had happened before, in other woods, happened now. The first moth that I had snared was a large one, and a specimen well worth securing. As I stretched out my hand to take it, the apparition of a flying shadow passed, swift and noiseless, between me and the tree. In less than an instant the

1

insect was snatched away, when my fingers were within an inch of it. The bat had begun his supper, and the man and the mixture had provided it for him.

Out of five moths caught, I became the victim of clever theft in the case of three. The other two, of no great value as specimens, I was just quick enough to secure. Under other circumstances, my patience as a collector would still have been a match for the dexterity of the bats. But on that evening – a memorable evening when I look back at it now – my spirits were depressed, and I was easily discouraged. My favourite studies of the insect-world seemed to have lost their value in my estimation. In the silence and the darkness I lay down under a tree, and let my mind dwell on myself and on my new life to come.

I am Gerard Roylake, son and only child of the late Gerard Roylake of Trimley Deen.

At twenty-two years of age, my father's death had placed me in possession of his large landed property. On my arrival from Germany, only a few hours since, the servants innocently vexed me. When I drove up to the door, I heard them say to each other: 'Here is the young Squire.' My father used to be called 'the old Squire'. I shrank from being reminded of him – not as other sons in my position might have said, because it renewed my sorrow for his death. There was no sorrow in me to be renewed. It is a shocking confession to make: my heart remained unmoved when I thought of the father whom I had lost.

Our mothers have the most sacred of all claims on our gratitude and our love. They have nourished us with their blood; they have risked their lives in bringing us into the world; they have preserved and guided our helpless infancy with divine patience and love. What claim equally strong and equally tender does the other parent establish on his offspring? What motive does the instinct of his young children find for preferring their father before any other person who may be a familiar object in their daily lives? They love him – naturally and rightly love him – because he lives in their remembrance (if he is a good man) as the first, the best, the dearest of their friends.

My father was a bad man. He was my mother's worst enemy; and he was never my friend.

The little that I know of the world tells me that it is not the common lot in life of women to marry the object of their first love. A sense of duty had compelled my mother to part with the man who had won her heart, in the first days of her maidenhood; and my father had discovered it, after his marriage. His insane jealousy, foully wronged the truest wife, the most long-suffering woman that ever lived. I have no patience to write of it. For ten miserable years she suffered her martyrdom; she lived through it, dear angel, sweet suffering soul, for my sake. At her death, my father was able to gratify his hatred of the son whom he had never believed to be his own child. Under pretence of preferring the foreign system of teaching, he sent me to a school in France. My education having been so far completed, I was next transferred to a German University. Never again did I see the place of my birth, never did I get a letter from home, until the family lawyer wrote from Trimley Deen, requesting me to assume possession of my house and lands, under the entail.

I should not even have known that my father had taken a second wife but for some friend (or enemy) – I never discovered the person – who sent me a newspaper containing an announcement of the marriage.

When we saw each other for the first time, my stepmother and I met necessarily as strangers. We were elaborately polite, and we each made a meritorious effort to appear at our ease. On her side, she found herself confronted by a young man, the new master of the house, who looked more like a foreigner than an Englishman – who, when he was congratulated (in view of the approaching season) on the admirable preservation of his partridges and pheasants, betrayed an utter want of interest in the subject; and who showed no sense of shame in acknowledging that his principal amusements were derived from reading books, and collecting insects. How I must have disappointed Mrs Roylake! and how considerately she hid from me the effect that I had produced!

Turning next to my own impressions, I discovered in my newly-found relative, a little light-eyed, light-haired, elegant woman; trim, and bright, and smiling; dressed to perfection,

clever to her fingers' ends, skilled in making herself agreeable
– and yet, in spite of these undeniable fascinations, perfectly
incomprehensible to me. After my experience of foreign
society, I was incapable of understanding the extraordinary
importance which my stepmother seemed to attach to rank
and riches, entirely for their own sakes. When she described
my unknown neighbours, from one end of the county to the
other, she took it for granted that I must be interested in them
on account of their titles and their fortunes. She held me up to
my own face, as a kind of idol to myself, without producing
any better reason than might be found in my inheritance of an
income of sixteen thousand pounds. And when I expressed (in
excusing myself for not accompanying her, uninvited, to the
dinner-party) a perfectly rational doubt whether I might prove
to be a welcome guest, Mrs Roylake held up her delicate little
hands in unutterable astonishment. 'My dear Gerard, in *your*
position!' She appeared to think that this settled the question. I
submitted in silence; the truth is, I was beginning already to
despair of my prospects. Kind as my stepmother was, and
agreeable as she was, what chance could I see of establishing
any true sympathy between us? And, if my neighbours
resembled her in their ways of thinking, what hope could I feel
of finding new friends in England to replace the friends in
Germany whom I had lost? A stranger among my own
country people, with the every-day habits and every-day
pleasures of my youthful life left behind me – without plans or
hopes to interest me in looking at the future – it is surely not
wonderful that my spirits had sunk to their lowest ebb, and
that I even failed to appreciate with sufficient gratitude the
fortunate accident of my birth.

Perhaps the journey to England had fatigued me, or perhaps
the controlling influences of the dark and silent night proved
irresistible. This only is certain: my solitary meditations under
the tree ended in sleep.

I was awakened by a light falling on my face.

The moon had risen. In the outward part of the wood,
beyond which I had not advanced, the pure and welcome light
penetrated easily through the scattered trees. I got up and
looked about me. A path into the wood now showed itself,
broader and better kept than any path that I could remember

in the days of my boyhood. The moon showed it to me plainly, and my curiosity was aroused.

Following the new track, I found that it led to a little glade which I at once recognized. The place was changed in one respect only. A neglected water-spring had been cleared of brambles and stones, and had been provided with a drinking cup, a rustic seat, and a Latin motto on a marble slab. The spring at once reminded me of a greater body of water – a river, at some little distance farther on, which ran between the trees on one side, and the desolate open country on the other. Ascending from the glade, I found myself in one of the narrow woodland paths, familiar to me in the by-gone time.

Unless my memory was at fault, this was the way which led to an old water-mill on the river-bank. The image of the great turning wheel, which half-frightened half-fascinated me when I was a child, now presented itself to my memory for the first time after an interval of many years. In my present frame of mind, the old scene appealed to me with the irresistible influence of an old friend. I said to myself: 'Shall I walk on, and try if I can find the river and the mill again?' This perfectly trifling question to decide presented to me, nevertheless, fantastic difficulties so absurd that they might have been difficulties encountered in a dream. To my own astonishment, I hesitated – walked back again along the path by which I had advanced – reconsidered my decision, without knowing why – and turning in the opposite direction, set my face towards the river once more. I wonder how my life would have ended, if I had gone the other way?

CHAPTER II

THE RIVER INTRODUCES US

I stood alone on the bank of the ugliest stream in England.

The moonlight, pouring its unclouded radiance over open space, failed to throw a beauty not their own on those sluggish waters. Broad and muddy, their stealthy current flowed onward to the sea, without a rock to diversify, without a bubble to break, the sullen surface. On the side from which I was looking at the river, the neglected trees grew so close together that they were undermining their own lives, and poisoning each other. On the opposite bank, a rank growth of gigantic bulrushes hid the ground beyond, except where it rose in hillocks, and showed its surface of desert sand spotted here and there by mean patches of heath. A repellent river in itself, a repellent river in its surroundings, a repellent river even in its name. It was called The Loke. Neither popular tradition nor antiquarian research could explain what the name meant, or could tell when the name had been given. 'We call it The Loke; they do say no fish can live in it; and it dirties the clean salt water when it runs into the sea.' Such was the character of the river in the estimation of the people who knew it best. But I was pleased to see The Loke again. The ugly river, like the woodland glade, looked at me with the face of an old friend.

On my right hand side rose the venerable timbers of the water-mill.

The wheel was motionless, at that time of night; and the whole structure looked – as remembered objects will look, when we see them again after a long interval – smaller than I had supposed it to be. Otherwise, I could discover no change in the mill. But the wooden cottage attached to it had felt the devastating march of time. A portion of the decrepit building still stood revealed in its wretched old age; propped, partly by beams which reached from the thatched roof to the ground, and partly by the wall of a new cottage attached, presenting in yellow brick-work a hideous modern contrast to all that was left of its ancient neighbour.

Had the miller whom I remembered, died; and were these changes the work of his successor? I thought of asking the question, and tried the door: it was fastened. The windows were all dark excepting one, which I discovered in the upper storey, at the farther side of the new building. Here, there was a dim light burning. It was impossible to disturb a person, who, for all I knew to the contrary, might be going to bed. I turned back to The Loke, proposing to extend my walk, by a mile or a little more, to a village that I remembered on the bank of the river.

I had not advanced far, when the stillness around me was disturbed by an intermittent sound of splashing in the water. Pausing to listen, I heard next the working of oars in their rowlocks. After another interval a boat appeared, turning a projection in the bank, and rowed by a woman pulling steadily against the stream.

As the boat approached me in the moonlight, this person corrected my first impression, and revealed herself as a young girl. So far as I could perceive she was a stranger to me. Who could the girl be, alone on the river at that time of night? Idly curious I followed the boat, instead of pursuing my way to the village, to see whether she would stop at the mill, or pass it.

She stopped at the mill, secured the boat, and stepped on shore.

Taking a key from her pocket, she was about to open the door of the cottage, when I advanced and spoke to her. As far from recognizing her as ever, I found myself nevertheless thinking of an odd outspoken child, living at the mill in past years, who had been one of my poor mother's favourites at our village school. I ran the risk of offending her, by bluntly expressing the thought which was then in my mind.

'Is it possible that you are Cristel Toller?' I said.

The question seemed to amuse her. 'Why shouldn't I be Cristel Toller?' she asked.

'You were a little girl,' I explained, 'when I saw you last. You are so altered now – and so improved – that I should never have

guessed you might be the daughter of Giles Toller of the mill, if I
had not seen you opening the cottage door.'

She acknowledged my compliment by a curtsey, which
reminded me again of the village school. 'Thank you, young
man,' she said smartly; 'I wonder who you are?'

'Try if you can recollect me,' I suggested.

'May I take a long look at you?'

'As long as you like.'

She studied my face, with a mental effort to remember me,
which gathered her pretty eyebrows together quaintly in a
frown.

'There's something in his eyes,' she remarked, not speaking to
me but to herself, 'which doesn't seem to be quite strange. But I
don't know his voice, and I don't know his beard.' She
considered a little, and addressed herself directly to me once
more. 'Now I look at you again, you seem to be a gentleman. Are
you one?'

'I hope so.'

'Then you're not making game of me?'

'My dear, I am only trying if you can remember Gerard
Roylake.'

While in charge of the boat, the miller's daughter had been
rowing with bared arms; beautiful dusky arms, at once delicate
and strong. Thus far, she had forgotten to cover them up. The
moment I mentioned my name, she started back as if I had
frightened her – pulled her sleeves down in a hurry – and hid the
objects of my admiration as an act of homage to myself! Her
verbal apologies followed.

'You used to be such a sweet-spoken pretty little boy,' she
said, 'how should I know you again, with a big voice and all that
hair on your face?' It seemed to strike her on a sudden that she had
been too familiar. 'Oh, Lord,' I heard her say to herself, 'half the
county belongs to him!' She tried another apology, and hit this
time on the conventional form. 'I beg your pardon, sir. Welcome
back to your own country, sir. I wish you good-night, sir.'

She attempted to escape into the cottage; I followed her to the
threshold of the door. 'Surely it's not time to go to bed yet,' I
ventured to say.

She was still on her good behaviour to her landlord. 'Not if
you object to it, sir,' she answered.

This recognition of my authority was irresistible. Cristel had laid me under an obligation to her good influence for which I felt sincerely grateful – she had made me laugh, for the first time since my return to England.

'We needn't say good-night just yet,' I suggested; 'I want to hear a little more about you. Shall I come in?'

She stepped out of the doorway even more rapidly than she had stepped into it. I might have been mistaken, but I thought Cristel seemed to be actually alarmed by my proposal. We walked up and down the river-bank. On every occasion when we approached the cottage, I detected her in stealing a look at the ugly modern part of it. There could be no mistake this time; I saw doubt, I saw anxiety in her face. What was going on at the mill? I made some domestic inquiries, beginning with her father. Was the miller alive and well?

'Oh yes, sir. Father gets thinner as he gets older – that's all.'

'Did he send you out by yourself, at this late hour, in the boat?'

'They were waiting for a sack of flour down there,' she replied, pointing in the direction of the river-side village. 'Father isn't as quick as he used to be. He's often late over his work now.'

Was there no one to give Giles Toller the help that he must need at his age? 'Do you and your father really live alone in this solitary place?' I said.

A change of expression appeared in her bright brown eyes which roused my curiosity. I also observed that she evaded a direct reply. 'What makes you doubt, sir, if father and I live alone?' she asked.

I pointed to the new cottage. 'That ugly building,' I answered, 'seems to give you more room than you want – unless there is somebody else living at the mill.'

I had no intention of trying to force the reply from her which she had hitherto withheld; but she appeared to put that interpretation on what I had said. 'If you will have it,' she burst out, 'there *is* somebody else living with us.'

'A man who helps your father?'

'No. A man who pays my father's rent.'

I was quite unprepared for such a reply as this: Cristel had surprised me. To begin with, her father was 'well-connected,' as we say in England. His younger brother had made a fortune in commerce, and had vainly offered him the means of retiring from the mill with a sufficient income. Then again, Giles Toller was known to have saved money. His domestic expenses made no heavy demand on his purse; his German wife (whose Christian name was now borne by his daughter) had died long since; his sons were no burden on him; they had never lived at the mill in my remembrance. With all these reasons against his taking a stranger into his house, he had nevertheless, if my interpretation of Cristel's answer was the right one, let his spare rooms to a lodger. 'Mr Toller can't possibly be in want of money,' I said.

'The more money father has, the more he wants. That's the reason,' she added bitterly, 'why he asked for plenty of room when the cottage was built, and why we have got a lodger.'

'Is the lodger a gentleman?'

'I don't know. Is a man a gentleman, if he keeps a servant? Oh, don't trouble to think about it, sir! It isn't worth thinking about.'

This was plain speaking at last. 'You don't seem to like the lodger,' I said.

'I hate him!'

'Why?'

She turned on me with a look of angry amazement — not undeserved, I must own, on my part — which showed her dark beauty in the perfection of its lustre and its power. To my eyes she was at the moment irresistibly charming. I daresay I was blind to the defects in her face. My good German tutor used to lament that there was too much of my boyhood still left in me. Honestly admiring her, I let my favourable opinion express itself a little too plainly. 'What a splendid creature you are!' I burst out. Cristel did her duty to herself and to me; she passed over my little explosion of nonsense without taking the smallest notice of it.

'Master Gerard,' she began — and checked herself. 'Please to excuse me, sir; you have set my head running on old times. What I want to say is: you were not so inquisitive when you were a young gentleman in short jackets. Please behave as you used to behave then, and don't say anything more about our lodger. I hate him because I hate him. There!'

Ignorant as I was of the natures of women, I understood her at last. Cristel's opinion of the lodger was evidently the exact opposite of the lodger's opinion of Cristel. When I add that this discovery did decidedly operate as a relief to my mind, the impression produced on me by the miller's daughter is stated without exaggeration and without reserve.

'Good-night,' she repeated, 'for the last time.' I held out my hand. 'Is it quite right, sir,' she modestly objected, 'for such as me to shake hands with such as you?'

She did it nevertheless; and dropping my hand, cast a farewell look at the mysterious object of her interest – the new cottage. Her variable humour changed on the instant. Apparently in a state of unendurable irritation, she stamped on the ground. 'Just what I didn't want to happen!' she said to herself.

CHAPTER III

HE SHOWS HIMSELF

I too, looked at the cottage, and made a discovery that surprised me at one of the upper windows.

If I could be sure that the moon had not deceived me, the most beautiful face that I had ever seen was looking down on us – and it was the face of a man! By the uncertain light I could discern the perfection of form in the features, and the expression of power which made it impossible to mistake the stranger for a woman, although his hair grew long and he was without either moustache or beard. He was watching us intently; he neither moved nor spoke when we looked up at him.

'Evidently the lodger,' I whispered to Cristel. 'What a handsome man!'

She tossed her head contemptuously: my expression of admiration seemed to have irritated her.

'I didn't want him to see you!' she said. 'The lodger persecutes me with his attentions; he's impudent enough to be jealous of me.'

She spoke without even attempting to lower her voice. I endeavoured to warn her. 'He's at the window still,' I said, in tones discreetly lowered; 'he can hear everything you are saying.'

'Not one word of it, Mr Gerard.'

'What do you mean?'

'The man is deaf. Don't look at him again. Don't speak to me again. Go home – pray go home!'

Without further explanation, she abruptly entered the cottage, and shut the door.

As I turned into the path which led through the wood I heard a voice behind me. It said: 'Stop, sir.' I stopped directly,

12

standing in the shadow cast by the outermost line of trees, which I had that moment reached. In the moonlight that I had left behind me, I saw again the man whom I had discovered at the window. His figure, tall and slim; his movements, graceful and easy, were in harmony with his beautiful face. He lifted his long finely-shaped hands, and clasped them with a frantic gesture of entreaty.

'For God's sake,' he said, 'don't be offended with me!'

His voice startled me even more than his words; I had never heard anything like it before. Low, dull, and muffled, it neither rose nor fell; it spoke slowly and deliberately, without laying the slightest emphasis on any one of the words that it uttered. In the astonishment of the moment, I forgot what Cristel had told me. I answered him as I should have answered any other unknown person who had spoken to me.

'What do you want?'

His hands dropped; his head sunk on his breast. 'You are speaking, sir, to a miserable creature who can't hear you. I am deaf.'

I stepped nearer to him, intending to raise my voice in pity for his infirmity. He shuddered, and signed to me to keep back.

'Don't come close to my ear; don't shout.' As he spoke, strong excitement flashed at me in his eyes, without producing the slightest change in his voice. 'I don't deny,' he resumed, 'that I can hear sometimes when people take that way with me. They hurt when they do it. Their voices go through my nerves as a knife might go through my flesh. I live at the mill, sir; I have ? great favour to ask. Will you come and speak to me in my room – for five minutes only?'

I hesitated. Any other man in my place, would, I think, have done the same; receiving such an invitation as this from a stranger, whose pitiable infirmity seemed to place him beyond the pale of social intercourse.

He must have guessed what was passing in my mind; he tried me again in words which might have proved persuasive, had they been uttered in the customary variety of tone.

'I can't help being a stranger to you; I can't help being deaf. You're a young man. You look more merciful and more patient than young men in general. Won't you hear what I have to say? Won't you tell me what I want to know?'

How were we to communicate? Did he by any chance suppose that I had learnt the finger alphabet? I touched my fingers and shook my head, as a means of dissipating his delusion, if it existed.

He instantly understood me.

'Even if you knew the finger alphabet,' he said, 'it would be of no use. I have been too miserable to learn it – my deafness only came on me a little more than a year since. Pardon me if I am obliged to give you trouble – I ask persons who pity me to write their answers when I speak to them. Come to my room, and you will find what you want – a candle to write by.'

Was his will, as compared with mine, the stronger will of the two? And was it helped (insensibly to myself) by his advantages of personal appearance? I can only confess that his apology presented a picture of misery to my mind, which shook my resolution to refuse him. His ready penetration discovered this change in his favour: he at once took advantage of it. 'Five minutes of your time is all I ask for,' he said. 'Won't you indulge a man who sees his fellow-creatures all talking happily round him, and feels dead and buried among them?'

The very exaggeration of his language had its effect on my mind. It revealed to me the horrible isolation among humanity of the deaf, as I had never understood it yet. Discretion is, I am sorry to say, not one of the strong points in my character. I committed one more among the many foolish actions of my life; I signed to the stranger to lead the way back to the mill.

CHAPTER IV

HE EXPLAINS HIMSELF

Giles Toller's miserly nature had offered to his lodger shelter from wind and rain, and the furniture absolutely necessary to make a bedroom habitable – and nothing more. There was no carpet on the floor, no paper on the walls, no ceiling to hide the rafters of the roof. The chair that I sat on was the one chair in the room; the man whose guest I had rashly consented to be found a seat on his bed. Upon his table I saw pens and pencils, paper and ink, and a battered brass candlestick with a common tallow candle in it. His changes of clothing were flung on the bed; his money was left on the unpainted wooden chimney-piece; his wretched little morsel of looking-glass (propped up near the money) had been turned with its face to the wall. He perceived that the odd position of this last object had attracted my notice.

'Vanity and I have parted company,' he explained; 'I shrink from myself when I look at myself now. The ugliest man living – if he has got his hearing – is a more agreeable man in society than I am. Does this wretched place disgust you?'

He pushed a pencil and some sheets of writing-paper across the table to me. I wrote my reply: 'The place makes me sorry for you.'

He shook his head. 'Your sympathy is thrown away on me. A man who has lost his social relations with his fellow-creatures doesn't care how he lodges or where he lives. When he has found solitude, he has found all he wants for the rest of his days. Shall we introduce ourselves? It won't be easy for me to set the example.'

I used the pencil again: 'Why not?'

'Because you will expect me to give you my name. I can't do it. I have ceased to bear my family name; and, being out of society, what need have I for an assumed name? As for my Christian name, it's so detestably ugly that I hate the sight and sound of it. Here, they know me as The Lodger. Will you have that? or will you have an appropriate nick-name? I come of a mixed breed; and I'm likely, after what has happened to me, to turn out a worthless fellow. Call me The Cur. Oh, you needn't start! that's as accurate a description of me as any other. What's *your* name?'

I wrote it for him. His face darkened when he found out who I was.

'Young, personally attractive, and a great landowner,' he said. 'I saw you just now talking familiarly with Cristel Toller. I didn't like that at the time; I like it less than ever now.'

My pencil asked him, without ceremony, what he meant.

He was ready with his reply. 'I mean this: you owe something to the good luck which has placed you where you are. Keep your familiarity for ladies in your own rank of life.'

This (to a young man like me) was unendurable insolence. I had hitherto refrained from taking him at his own bitter word in the matter of nick-name. In the irritation of the moment, I now first resolved to adopt his suggestion seriously. The next slip of paper that I handed to him administered the smartest rebuff that my dull brains could discover on the spur of the moment: 'The Cur is requested to keep his advice till he is asked for it.'

For the first time, something like a smile showed itself faintly on his lips – and represented the only effect which my severity had produced. He still followed his own train of thought, as resolutely and as impertinently as ever.

'I haven't seen you talking to Cristel before to-night. Have you been meeting her in secret?'

In justice to the girl, I felt that I ought to set him right, so far. Taking up the pencil again, I told this strange man that I had just returned to England, after an absence of many years in foreign countries – that I had known Cristel when we were both children – and that I had met her purely by accident, when he had detected us talking outside the cottage. Seeing me pause, after advancing to that point in the writing of my reply, he held out his hand impatiently for the paper. I signed him to wait, and added a last sentence: 'Understand this; I will answer no more questions – I have done with the subject.'

He read what I had written with the closest attention. But his inveterate suspicion of me was not set at rest, even yet.

'Are you likely to come this way again?' he asked.

I pointed to the final lines of my writing, and got up to go.

This assertion of my will against his roused him. He stopped me at the door – not by a motion of his hand but by the mastery of his look. The dim candlelight afforded me no help in determining the colour of his eyes. Dark, large, and finely set in his head, there was a sinister passion in them, at that moment, which held me in spite of myself. Still as monotonous as ever, his voice in some degree expressed the frenzy that was in him, by suddenly rising in its pitch when he spoke to me next.

'Mr Roylake, I love her. Mr Roylake, I am determined to marry her. Any man who comes between me and that cruel girl – ah, she's as hard as one of her father's millstones; it's the misery of my life, it's the joy of my life, to love her – I tell you, young sir, any man who comes between Cristel and me does it at his peril. Remember that.'

I had no wish to give offence – but his threatening me in this manner was so absurd that I gave way to the impression of the moment, and laughed. He stepped up to me, with such an expression of demoniacal rage and hatred in his face that he became absolutely ugly in an instant.

'I amuse you, do I?' he said. 'You don't know the man you're trifling with. You had better know me. You *shall* know me.' He turned away, and walked up and down the wretched little room, deep in thought. 'I don't want this matter between us to end badly,' he said, interrupting his meditations – then returning to them again – and then once more addressing me. 'You're young, you're thoughtless; but you don't look like a bad fellow. I wonder whether I can trust you? Not one man in a thousand would do it. Never mind. I'm the one man in ten thousand who does it. Mr Gerard Roylake, I'm going to trust you.'

With this incoherent expression of a resolution unknown to me, he unlocked a shabby trunk hidden in a corner, and took from it a small portfolio.

'Men of your age,' he resumed, 'seldom look below the surface. Learn that valuable habit, sir – and begin by looking below the surface of Me.' He forced the portfolio into my hand. Once more, his beautiful eyes held me with their irresistible influence; they looked at me with an expression of sad and solemn warning. 'Discover for yourself,' he said, 'what devils my deafness has set loose in me; and let no eyes but yours see that horrid sight. You will find me here to-morrow, and you will decide by that time whether you make an enemy of me or not.'

He threw open the door, and bowed as graciously as if he had been a sovereign dismissing a subject.

Was he mad?

I hesitated to adopt that conclusion. There is no denying it, the deaf man had found his own strange and tortuous way to my interest, in spite of myself. I might even have been in some danger of allowing him to make a friend of me, if I had not been restrained by the fears for Cristel which his language and his manner amply justified, to my mind. Although I was far from foreseeing the catastrophe that really did happen, I felt that I had returned to my own country at a critical time in the life of the miller's daughter. My friendly interference might be of serious importance to Cristel's peace of mind – perhaps even to her personal safety as well.

Eager to discover what the contents of the portfolio might tell me, I hurried back to Trimley Deen. My stepmother had not yet returned from the dinner-party. As one of the results of my ten years' banishment from home, I was obliged to ask the servant to show me the way to my own room, in my own house! The windows looked out on a view of Fordwitch Wood. As I opened the leaves which were to reveal to me the secret soul of the man whom I had so strangely met, the fading moonlight vanished, and the distant trees were lost in the gloom of a starless night.

CHAPTER V

HE BETRAYS HIMSELF

The confession was entitled, 'Memoirs of a Miserable Man'. It began abruptly in these words:

I

'I acknowledge, at the outset, that misfortune has had an effect on me which frail humanity is for the most part anxious to conceal. Under the influence of suffering, I have become of enormous importance to myself. In this frame of mind, I naturally enjoy painting my own portrait in words. Let me add that they must be written words because it is a painful effort to me (since I lost my hearing) to speak to anyone continuously, for any length of time.

'I have also to confess that my brains are not so completely under my own command as I could wish.

'For instance, I possess considerable skill (for an amateur) as a painter in water colours. But I can only produce a work of art, when irresistible impulse urges me to express my thoughts in form and colour. The same obstacle to regular exertion stands in my way, if I am using my pen. I can only write when the fit takes me – sometimes at night when I ought to be asleep; sometimes at meals when I ought to be handling my knife and fork; sometimes out of doors when I meet with inquisitive strangers who stare at me. As for paper, the first stray morsel of anything that I can write upon will do, provided I snatch it up in time to catch my ideas as they fly.

'My method being now explained, I proceed to the deliberate act of self-betrayal which I contemplate in producing this picture of myself.

19

II

'I divide my life into two Epochs – respectively entitled: Before my Deafness, and After my Deafness. Or, suppose I define the melancholy change in my fortunes more sharply still, by contrasting with each other my days of prosperity and my days of disaster? Of these alternatives, I hardly know which to choose. It doesn't matter; the one thing needful is to go on.

'In any case, then, I have to record that I passed a happy childhood – thanks to my good mother. Her generous nature had known adversity, and had not been deteriorated by undeserved trials. Born of slave-parents, she had not reached her eighteenth year, when she was sold by auction in the Southern States of America. The person who bought her (she never would tell me who he was) freed her by a codicil, added to his will on his deathbed. My father met with her, a few years afterwards, in American society – fell (as I have heard) madly in love with her – and married her in defiance of the wishes of his family. He was quite right: no better wife and mother ever lived. The one vestige of good feeling that I still possess, lives in my empty heart when I dwell at times on the memory of my mother.

'My good fortune followed me when I was sent to school.

'Our head master was more nearly a perfect human being than any other man that I have ever met with. Even the worst-tempered boys among us ended in loving him. Under his encouragement, and especially to please him, I won every prize that industry, intelligence, and good conduct could obtain; and I rose, at an unusually early age, to be the head boy in the first class. When I was old enough to be removed to the University, and when the dreadful day of parting arrived, I fainted under the agony of leaving the teacher – no! the dear friend – whom I devotedly loved. There must surely have been some good in me at that time. What has become of it now?

'The years followed each other – and I was Fortune's spoilt child still.

'Under adverse circumstances, my sociable disposition, my delight in the society of young people of my own age, might have exposed me to serious dangers in my new sphere of action. Happily for me, my father consulted a wise friend, before he sent me to Cambridge. I was entered at one of the smaller colleges; and I fell, at starting, among the right set of men. Good examples were all round me. We formed a little club of steady students; our pleasures were innocent; we were too proud and too poor to get into debt. I look back on my career at Cambridge, as I look back on my career at school, and wonder what has become of my better self.

III

'During my last year at Cambridge, my father died.

'The profession which he had intended that I should follow was the Bar. I believed myself to be quite unfit for the sort of training imperatively required by the Law; and my mother agreed with me. When I left the University, my own choice of a profession pointed to the medical art, and to that particular branch of it called surgery. After three years of unremitting study at one of the great London hospitals, I started in practice for myself. Once more, my persistent luck was faithful to me at the outset of my new career.

'The winter of that year was remarkable for alternate extremes of frost and thaw. Accidents to passengers in the streets were numerous; and one of them happened close to my own door. A gentleman slipped on the icy pavement, and broke his leg. On sending news of the accident to his house, I found that my chance-patient was a nobleman.

'My lord was so well satisfied with my services that he refused to be attended by any of my elders and betters in the profession. Little did I think at the time, that I had received the last of the favours which Fortune was to bestow on me. I enjoyed the confidence and goodwill of a man possessing boundless social influence; and I was received most kindly by the ladies of his family. In one word, at the time when my professional prospects justified the brightest hopes that I could form, sudden death deprived me of the dearest and truest of all friends – I suffered the one dreadful loss which it is impossible to replace, the loss of my mother. We had parted at night when she was, to all appearance, in the enjoyment of her customary health. The next morning, she was found dead in her bed.

IV

'Keen observers, who read these lines, will remark that I have said nothing about the male members of my family, and that I have even passed over my father with the briefest possible allusion to his death.

'This curious reticence on my part, is simply attributable to pure ignorance. Until affliction lay heavy on me, my father, my uncle, and my grandfather were hardly better known to me, in their true characters, than if they had been strangers passing in the street. How I contrived to become more intimately acquainted with my ancestors, I am now to reveal.

'In the absence of any instructions to guide me, after my mother's death, I was left to use my own discretion in examining the papers which she had left behind her. Reading her letters carefully, before I decided what to keep and what to destroy, I discovered a packet, protected by an unbroken seal, and bearing an inscription, addressed abruptly to my mother in these words:

'For fear of accidents, my dear, we will mention no names in this place. The sight of my handwriting will remind you of my devotion to your interests in the past, and will satisfy you that I am to be trusted in the service that I now offer to my good sister-friend. In the fewest words, let me tell you that I have heard of the circumstances under which your marriage has taken place. Your origin has unfortunately become known to the members of your husband's family; their pride has been deeply wounded; and the women especially regard you with feelings of malignant hatred. I have good reason for fearing that they may try to excuse their inhuman way of speaking of you, by making public the calamity of your slave-birth. What deplorable influence might be exercised on your husband's mind, by such an exposure as this, I will not stop to inquire. It will be more to the purpose to say that I am able to offer you a sure means of protecting yourself – through information which I have unexpectedly obtained, and the source of which I am obliged to keep secret. If you are ever threatened by your enemies, open the packet which I have now sealed up, and you will command the silence of the bitterest man or woman who longs to injure you. I may add that absolute proof accompanies every assertion which my packet contains. Keep it carefully, as long as you live – and God grant you may never have occasion to break the seal.

'Such was the inscription; copied exactly, word for word.

'I cannot even guess who my mother's devoted friend may have been. Neither can I doubt that she would have destroyed the packet, but for the circumstance of her sudden death.

'After hesitating a little – I hardly know why – I summoned my resolution, and broke the seal. Of the horror with which I read the contents of the packet I shall say nothing. Who ever yet sympathized with the sorrows and sufferings of strangers? Let me merely announce that I knew my ancestors at last, and that I am now able to present them in their true characters, as follows:

V

'My grandfather was tried on a charge of committing wilful murder – was found guilty on the clearest evidence – and died on the scaffold by the hangman's hands.

'His two sons abandoned the family name, and left the family residence. They were, nevertheless, not unworthy representatives of their atrocious father, as will presently appear.

'My uncle (a captain in the Army) was discovered at the hazard table, playing with loaded dice. Before this abject scoundrel could be turned out of his regiment, he was killed in a duel by one of his brother officers whom he had cheated.

'My father, when he was little more than a lad, deserted a poor girl who had trusted him under a promise of marriage. Friendless and hopeless, she drowned herself and her child. His was the most infamous in the list of the family crimes – and *he* escaped, without answering to a court of law or a court of honour for what he had done.

'Some of us come of one breed, and some of another. There is the breed from which I drew the breath of life. What do you think of me now?

VI

'I looked back over the past years of my existence, from the time of my earliest recollections to the miserable day when I opened the sealed packet.

'What wholesome influences had preserved me, so far, from moral contamination by the vile blood that ran in my veins? There were two answers to that question which, in some degree, quieted my mind. In the first place, resembling my good mother physically, I might hope to have resembled her morally. In the second place, the happy accidents of my career had preserved me from temptation, at more than one critical period of my life. On the other hand, in the ordinary course of nature, not one half of that life had yet elapsed. What trials might the future have in store for me? and what protection against them would the better part of my nature be powerful enough to afford?

'While I was still troubled by these doubts, the measure of my disasters was filled by an attack of illness which threatened me with death. My medical advisers succeeded in saving my life – and left me to pay the penalty of their triumph by the loss of one of my senses.

'At an early period of my convalescence, I noticed one day, with languid surprise, that the voices of the doctors, when they asked me how I had slept and if I felt better, sounded singularly dull and distant. A few hours later, I observed that they stooped close over me when they had something important to say. On the same evening, my day nurse and my night nurse happened to be in the room together. To my surprise, they had become so wonderfully quiet in their movements, that they opened the door or stirred the fire, without making the slightest noise. I intended to ask them what it meant; I had even begun to put the question, when I was startled by another discovery relating this time to myself. I was certain that I had spoken – and yet, I had not heard myself speak! As well as my weakness would let me, I called to the nurses in my loudest tones. "Has anything happened to my voice?" I asked. The two women consulted together, looking at me with pity in their eyes. One of them took the responsibility on herself.

She put her lips close to my ear; the horrid words struck me
with a sense of physical pain: "Your illness has left you in a sad
state, sir. You are deaf."

VII

'As soon as I was able to leave my bed, well-meaning people,
in and out of the medical profession, combined to torment me
with the best intentions.

'One famous aural surgeon after another came to me, and
quoted his experience of cases, in which the disease that had
struck me down had affected the sense of hearing in other
unhappy persons: they had submitted to surgical treatment,
generally with cheering results. I submitted in my turn. All
that skill could do for me was done, and without effect. My
deafness steadily increased; my case was pronounced to be
hopeless; the great authorities retired.

'Judicious friends, who had been waiting for their opportunity, undertook the moral management of me next.

'I was advised to cultivate cheerfulness, to go into society,
to encourage kind people who tried to make me hear what was
going on, to be on my guard against morbid depression, to
check myself when the sense of my own horrible isolation
drove me away to my room, and, last but by no means least,
to beware of letting my vanity disincline me to use an
ear-trumpet.

'I did my best, honestly did my best, to profit by the
suggestions that were offered to me – not because I believed in
the wisdom of my friends, but because I dreaded the effect of
self-imposed solitude on my nature. Since the fatal day when I
had opened the sealed packet, I was on my guard against the
inherited evil lying dormant, for all I knew to the contrary, in
my father's son. Impelled by that horrid dread, I suffered my
daily martyrdom with a courage that astonishes me when I
think of it now.

'What the self-inflicted torture of the deaf is, none but the
deaf can understand.

'When benevolent persons did their best to communicate to
me what was clever or amusing, while conversation was
going on in my presence, I was secretly angry with them for

making my infirmity conspicuous, and directing the general attention to me. When other friends saw in my face that I was not grateful to them, and gave up the attempt to help me, I suspected them of talking of me contemptuously, and amusing themselves by making my misfortune the subject of coarse jokes.

'Even when I deserved encouragement by honestly trying to atone for my bad behaviour, I committed mistakes (arising out of my helpless position) which prejudiced people against me. Sometimes, I asked questions which appeared to be so trivial, to ladies and gentlemen happy in the possession of a sense of hearing, that they evidently thought me imbecile as well as deaf. Sometimes, seeing the company enjoying an interesting story or a good joke, I ignorantly appealed to the most incompetent person present to tell me what had been said – with this result, that he lost the thread of the story or missed the point of the joke, and blamed my unlucky interference as the cause of it.

'These mortifications, and many more, I suffered patiently until, little by little, my last reserves of endurance felt the cruel strain on them, and failed me. My friends detected a change in my manner which alarmed them. They took me away from London, to try the renovating purity of country air.

'So far as any curative influence over the state of my mind was concerned, the experiment proved to be a failure.

'I had secretly arrived at the conclusion that my deafness was increasing, and that my friends knew it and were concealing it from me. Determined to put my suspicions to the test, I took long solitary walks in the neighbourhood of my country home, and tried to hear the new sounds about me. I was deaf to everything – with the one exception of the music of the birds.

'How long did I hear the little cheering songsters who comforted me?

'I am unable to measure the interval that elapsed: my memory fails me. I only know that the time came, when I could see the skylark in the heavens, but could no longer hear its joyous notes. In a few weeks more the nightingale, and even the loud thrush, became silent birds to my doomed ears. My last effort to resist my own deafness was made at my bedroom window. For some time I still heard, faintly and more faintly, the shrill twittering just above me, under the eaves of the house. When this last poor enjoyment came to an end – when I listened eagerly, desperately, and heard nothing (think of it, *nothing!*) – I gave up the struggle. Persuasions, arguments, entreaties were entirely without effect on me. Reckless what came of it, I retired to the one fit place for me – to the solitude in which I have buried myself ever since.

VIII

'With some difficulty, I discovered the lonely habitation of which I was in search.

'No language can describe the heavenly composure of mind that came to me, when I first found myself alone; living the death-in-life of deafness, apart from creatures – no longer my fellow-creatures – who could hear: apart also from those privileged victims of hysterical impulse, who wrote me love-letters, and offered to console the 'poor beautiful deaf man' by marrying him. Through the distorting medium of such sufferings as I have described, women and men – even young women – were repellent to me alike. Ungratefully impatient of the admiration excited by my personal advantages, savagely irritated by tender looks and flattering compliments, I only consented to take lodgings, on condition that there should be no young women living under the same roof with me. If this confession of morbid feeling looks like vanity, I can only say that appearances lie. I write in sober sadness; determined to present my character, with photographic accuracy, as a true likeness.

'What were my habits in solitude? How did I get through the weary and wakeful hours of the day?

'Living by myself, I became (as I have already acknowledged) important to myself – and, as a necessary consequence, I enjoyed registering my own daily doings. Let passages copied from my journal reveal how I got through the day.

IX

EXTRACTS FROM A DEAF MAN'S DIARY

'Monday. – Six weeks to-day since I first occupied my present retreat.

'My landlord and landlady are two hideous old people. They look as if they disliked me, on the rare occasions when we meet. So much the better; they don't remind me of my deafness by trying to talk, and they keep as much as possible out of my way. This morning, after breakfast, I altered the arrangement of my books – and then I made my fourth attempt, in the last ten days, to read some of my favourite authors. No: my taste has apparently changed since the time when I could hear. I closed one volume after another; caring nothing for what used to be deeply interesting to me.

'Reckless and savage – with a burning head and a cold heart – I went out to look about me.

'After two hours of walking and thinking, I found that I had wandered to our county town. The rain began to fall heavily just as I happened to be passing a bookseller's shop. After some hesitation – for I hate exposing my deafness to strangers – I asked leave to take shelter, and looked at the books.

'Among them was a collection of celebrated Trials. I thought of my grandfather; consulted the index; and, finding his name there, bought the work. The shopman (as I could guess from his actions and looks) proposed sending the parcel to me. I insisted on taking it away. The sky had cleared; and I was eager to read the details of my grandfather's crime.

'Tuesday. – Sat up late last night, reading my new book. My favourite poets, novelists, and historians have failed to interest me. I devoured the Trials with breathless delight; beginning of course with the murder in which I felt a family interest. Prepared to find my grandfather a ruffian, I confess I was surprised by the discovery that he was also a fool. The officers of justice had no merit in tracing the crime to him; his own stupidity delivered him into their hands. I read the evidence twice over, and put myself in his position, and saw the means plainly by which he might have set discovery at defiance.

'In the Preface to the Trials I found an allusion, in terms of praise, to a work of the same kind, published in the French language. I wrote to London at once, and ordered the book.

'Wednesday. – Is there some mysterious influence, in the silent solitude of my life, that is hardening my nature? Is there something unnatural in the existence of a man who never hears a sound? Is there a moral sense that suffers when a bodily sense is lost?

'These questions have been suggested to me by an incident that happened this morning.

'Looking out of window, I saw a brutal carter, on the road before the house, beating an over-loaded horse. A year since I should have interfered to protect the horse, without a moment's hesitation. If the wretch had been insolent, I should have seized his whip, and applied the heavy handle of it to his own shoulders. In past days, I have been more than once fined by a magistrate (privately in sympathy with my offence) for assaults committed by me in the interests of helpless animals. What did I feel now? Nothing but a selfish sense of uneasiness, at having been accidentally witness of an act which disturbed my composure. I turned away, regretting that I had gone to the window and looked out.

'This was not an agreeable train of thought to follow. What could I do? I was answered by the impulse which commands me to paint.

'I sharpened my pencils, and opened my box of colours, and determined to produce a work of art. To my astonishment, the brutal figure of the carter forced its way into my memory again and again. I felt (without in the least knowing why) as if the one chance of getting rid of this curious incubus, was to put the persistent image of the man on paper. It was done mechanically, and yet done so well, that I was encouraged to add to the picture. I put in next the poor beaten horse (another good likeness!); and then I introduced a life-like portrait of myself, giving the man the sound thrashing that he had deserved. Strange to say, this representation of what I ought to have done, relieved my mind as if I had actually done it. I looked at the pre-eminent figure of myself, and felt good, and turned to my Trials, and read them over again, and liked them better than ever.

'Thursday. – The bookseller has found a second-hand copy of the French Trials, and has sent them to me (as he expresses it) "on approval".

'I more than approve – I admire; and I more than admire – I imitate. These criminal stories are told with a dramatic power, which has impelled me to try if I can rival the clever French narrative. I found a promising subject by putting myself in my grandfather's place, and tracing the means by which it had occurred to me that he might have escaped the discovery of his crime.

'I cannot remember having read any novel with a tenth part of the interest that absorbed me, in constructing my imaginary train of circumstances. So completely did the reality of the narrative impress itself on my mind, that I felt as if the murder that I was relating had been a crime committed by myself. It was my own ingenuity that hid the dead body, and removed the traces of blood – and my own self-control that presented me as an innocent person, when the victim was missing, and I was asked (among other respectable people) to say whether I thought he was living or dead.

'A whole week has passed – and has been occupied by my new literary pursuit.

'My inexhaustible imagination invents plots and conspir-acies of which I am the happy hero. I set traps which invariably catch my enemies. I place myself in positions which are entirely new to me. Yesterday, for instance, I invented a method of spiriting away a young person, whose dis-appearance was of considerable importance under the circum-stances, and succeeded in completely bewildering her father, her friends, and the police: not a trace of her could they find. If I ever have occasion to do, in reality, what I only suppose myself to do in these exercises of ingenuity, what a dangerous man I may yet prove to be!

'This morning, I rose, planning to amuse myself with a new narrative, when the ideal world in which I am now living, became a world annihilated by collision with the sordid interests of real life.

'In plainer words, I received a written message from my landlord which has annoyed me – and not without good cause. This tiresome person finds himself unexpectedly obliged to give up possession of his house. The circumstances are not worth relating. The result is important – I am compelled to find new lodgings. Where am I to go?

'I left it to chance. That is to say, I looked at the railway time-table, and took a ticket for the first place, of which the name happened to catch my eye. Arrived at my destination, I found myself in a dirty manufacturing town, with an ugly river running through it.

'After a little reflection, I turned my back on the town, and followed the course of the river, in search of shelter and solitude on one or the other of its banks. An hour of walking brought me to an odd-looking cottage, half old and half new, attached to a water-mill. A bill in one of the windows announced that rooms were to be let; and a look round revealed a thick wood on my left hand, and a wilderness of sand and heath on my right. So far as appearances went, here was the very place for me.

'I knocked at the door, and was admitted by a little lean shy-looking old man. He showed me the rooms – one for myself, and one for my servant. Wretched as they were, the loneliness of the situation recommended them to me. I made no objections; and I consented to pay the rent that was asked. The one thing that remained to be done, in the interests of my tranquillity, was to ascertain if any other persons lived in the cottage besides my new landlord. He wrote his answer to the question: "Nobody but my daughter." With serious misgivings, I inquired if his daughter was young. He wrote two fatal figures: "18."

'Here was a discovery which disarranged all my plans, just as I had formed them! The prospect of having a girl in the house, at the age associated with my late disagreeable experience of the sensitive sex, was more than my irritable temper could endure. I saw the old man going to the window to take down the bill. Turning in a rage to stop him, I was suddenly brought to a standstill by the appearance of a person who had just entered the room.

'Was this the formidable obstacle to my tranquillity, which had prevented me from taking the rooms that I had chosen? Yes! I knew the miller's daughter intuitively. Delirium possessed me; my eyes devoured her; my heart beat as if it would burst out of my bosom. The old man approached me; he nodded, and grinned, and pointed to her. Did he claim his parental interest in her? Did he mean that she belonged to him?

No! she belonged to me. She might be his daughter. She was My Fate.

'I don't know what it was in the girl that took me by storm. Nothing in her look or her manner expressed the slightest interest in me. That famous "beauty" of mine which had worked such ravages in the hearts of other young women, seemed not even to attract her notice. When her father put his hand to his ear, and told her (as I guessed) that I was deaf, there was no pity in her splendid brown eyes; they expressed a momentary curiosity, and nothing more. Possibly she had a hard heart? or perhaps she took a dislike to me, at first sight? It made no difference to my mind, either way. Was she the most beautiful creature I had ever seen? Not even that excuse was to be made for me. I have met with women of her dark complexion who were, beyond dispute her superiors in beauty, and have looked at them with indifference. Add to this, that I am one of the men whom women offend if they are not perfectly well-dressed. The miller's daughter was badly dressed; her magnificent figure was profaned by the wretchedly-made gown that she wore. I forgave the profanation. In spite of the protest of my own better taste, I resigned myself to her gown. Is it possible adequately to describe such infatuation as this? Quite possible! I have only to acknowledge that I took the rooms at the cottage – and there is the state of my mind, exposed without mercy!

'How will it end?'

CHAPTER VI

THE RETURN OF THE PORTFOLIO

With that serious question the last of the leaves entrusted to me by The Lodger at the Mill came to an end.

I betray no confidence in presenting this copy of his confession. Time has passed since I first read it, and changes have occurred in the interval, which leave me free to exercise my own discretion, and to let the autobiography speak for itself.

If I am asked what impression of the writer those extraordinary pages produced on me, I feel at a loss how to reply.

Not one impression, but many impressions, troubled and confused my mind. Certain passages in the confession inclined me to believe that the writer was mad. But I altered my opinion at the next leaf, and set him down as a man with a bitter humour, disposed to make merry over his own bad qualities. At one time, his tone in writing of his early life, and his allusions to his mother, won my sympathy and respect. At another time, the picture of himself in his later years, and the defiant manner in which he presented it, almost made me regret that he had not died of the illness which had struck him deaf. In this state of uncertainty I may claim the merit of having arrived, so far as my own future conduct was concerned, at one positive conclusion. As strangers he and I had first met. As strangers I was determined we should remain.

Having made up my mind, so far, the next thing to do (with the clock on the mantel-piece striking midnight) was to go to bed.

I slept badly. The events that had happened, since my arrival in England, had excited me I suppose. Now and then, in the wakeful hours of the night, I thought of Cristel with some anxiety. Taking The Lodger's exaggerated language for

33

what it was really worth, the poor girl (as I was still inclined to fear) might have serious reason to regret that he had ever entered her father's cottage.

At the breakfast table, my stepmother and I met again.

Mrs Roylake – in an exquisite morning dress; with her smile in perfect order – informed me that she was dying with curiosity. She had heard, from the servants, that I had not returned to the house until past ten o'clock on the previous night; and she was absolutely bewildered by the discovery. What could her dear Gerard have been doing, out in the dark by himself, for all that time?

'For some part of the time,' I answered, 'I was catching moths in Fordwitch Wood.'

'What an extraordinary occupation for a young man! Well? And what did you do after that?'

'I walked on through the wood, and renewed my old associations with the river and the mill.'

Mrs Roylake's fascinating smile disappeared when I mentioned the mill. She suddenly became a cold lady – I might even say a stiff lady.

'I can't congratulate you on the first visit you have paid in our neighbourhood,' she said. 'Of course that bold girl contrived to attract your notice?'

I replied that I had met with the 'bold girl' purely by accident, on her side as well as on mine; and then I started a new topic. 'Was it a pleasant dinner-party last night?' I asked – as if the subject really interested me. I had not been quite four and twenty hours in England yet, and I was becoming a humbug already.

My stepmother was her charming self again the moment my question had passed my lips. Society – provided it was not society at the mill – was always attractive as a topic of conversation. 'Your absence was the only drawback,' she answered. 'I have asked the two ladies (my lord has an engagement) to dine here to-day, without ceremony. They are most anxious to meet you. My dear Gerard! you look surprised. Surely you know who the ladies are?'

I was obliged to acknowledge my ignorance.

Mrs Roylake was shocked. 'At any rate,' she resumed, 'you have heard of their father, Lord Uppercliff?'

I made another shameful confession. Either I had forgotten Lord Uppercliff, during my long absence abroad, or I had never heard of him.

Mrs Roylake was disgusted. 'And this is a foreign education!' she exclaimed. 'Thank Heaven, you have returned to your own country! We will drive out after luncheon, and pay a round of visits.' When this prospect was placed before me, I remembered having read in books of sensitive persons receiving impressions which made their blood run cold; I now found myself one of those persons, for the first time in my life. 'In the meanwhile,' Mrs Roylake continued, 'I must tell you – excuse me for laughing; it seems so very absurd that you should not know who Lord Uppercliff's daughters are – I must tell you that Lady Rachel is the eldest. She is married to the Honourable Captain Millbay, of the Navy, now away in his ship. A person of extraordinary strength of mind (I don't mean the Captain; I mean Lady Rachel); I admire her intellect, but her political and social opinions I must always view with regret. Her younger sister, Lady Lena – not married, Gerard; remember that! – is simply the most charming girl in England. If you don't fall in love with her, you will be the only young man in the county who has resisted Lady Lena. Poor Sir George – she refused him last week; you really *must* have heard of Sir George; our member of parliament; conservative of course; quite broken-hearted about Lady Lena; gone away to America to shoot bears. You seem to be restless. What are you fidgeting about? Ah, I know! You want to smoke after breakfast. Well, I won't be in your way. Go out on the terrace; your poor father always took his cigar on the terrace. They say smoking leads to meditation; I leave you to meditate on Lady Lena. Don't forget – luncheon at one o'clock, and the carriage at two.'

She smiled, and kissed her hand, and fluttered out of the room. Charming; perfectly charming. And yet I was ungrateful enough to wish myself back in Germany again.

I lit my cigar, but not on the terrace. Leaving the house, I took the way once more that led to Fordwitch Wood. What would Mrs Roylake have said, if she had discovered that I was going back to the mill? There was no other alternative. The portfolio was a trust confided to me; the sooner I returned it to the writer of the confession – the sooner I told him plainly the conclusion at which I had arrived – the more at ease my mind would be.

The sluggish river looked muddier than ever, the new cottage looked uglier than ever, exposed to the searching ordeal of sunlight. I knocked at the door on the ancient side of the building.

Cristel's father – shall I confess I had hoped that it might be Cristel herself? – let me in. In by-gone days, I dimly remembered him as old and small and withered. Advancing years had wasted him away, in the interval, until his white miller's clothes hung about him in empty folds. His fleshless face would have looked like the face of a mummy, but for the restless brightness of his little watchful black eyes. He stared at me in momentary perplexity, and, suddenly recovering himself, asked me to walk in.

'Are you the young master, sir? Ah, yes, yes; I thought so. My girl Cristy said she saw the young master last night. Thank you kindly, sir; I'm pretty well, considering how I've fallen away in my flesh. I have got a fine appetite, but somehow or other, my meals don't show on me. You will excuse my receiving you in the kitchen, sir; it's the best room we have. Did Cristy tell you how badly we are off here for repairs? You being our landlord, we look to you to help us. We are falling to pieces, as it were, on this old side of the house. There's first the drains——'

He proceeded to reckon up the repairs, counting with his fleshless thumb on his skinny fingers, when he was interrupted by a curious succession of sounds which began with whining, and ended with scratching at the cottage door.

In a minute after, the door was opened from without. A brown dog, of the companionable retriever breed, ran in and fawned upon old Toller. Cristel followed (from the kitchen garden), with a basket of vegetables on her arm. Unlike the river and the cottage, she gained by being revealed in the brilliant sunlight. I now saw, in their full beauty, the lustre of her brown eyes, the warm rosiness of her dark complexion, the delightful vivacity of expression which was the crowning charm of her face. She paused confusedly in the doorway, and tried to resist me when I insisted on relieving her of the basket.

'Mr Gerard,' she protested, 'you are treating me as if I was a young lady. What would they say at the great house, if they knew you had done that?'

My answer would no doubt have assumed the form of a foolish compliment, if her father had not spared her that infliction. He returned to the all-important question, the question of repairs.

'You see, sir, it's no use speaking to the bailiff. Saving your presence, he's a miser with his master's money. He says, 'All right,' and he does nothing. There's first, as I told you just now, the truly dreadful state of the drains——'

I tried to stop him by promising to speak to the bailiff myself. On hearing this good news, Mr Toller's gratitude became ungovernable: he was more eager than ever, and more eloquent than ever, in returning to the repairs.

'And then, sir, there's the oven. They do call bread the staff of life. It's a burnt staff at one time, and a clammy staff at another, in our domestic experience. Satisfy yourself, sir; do please cross the kitchen and look with your own eyes at the state, the scandalous state, of the oven.'

His daughter interfered, and stopped him at the critical moment when he was actually offering his arm to conduct me in state across the kitchen. Cristel had just put her pretty brown hand over his mouth, and said, 'Oh, father, do pray be quiet!' when we were all three disturbed by another interruption.

A second door communicating, as I concluded from its position, with the new cottage, was suddenly opened. In the instant before the person behind it appeared, the dog looked that way – started up, frightened – and took refuge under the table. At the next moment, the deaf Lodger walked into the room. It was he beyond all doubt who had frightened the dog, forewarned by instinct of his appearance.

What I had read of his writing disposed me, now that I saw the man by daylight, to find something devilish in the expression of his face. No! strong as it was, my prejudice failed to make any discoveries that presented him at a disadvantage. His personal attractions triumphed in the clear searching light. I now perceived that his eyes were of that deeply dark blue, which is commonly and falsely described as resembling the colour of the violet. To my thinking, they were so entirely beautiful that they had no right to be in a man's face. I might have felt the same objection to the pale delicacy of his complexion, to the soft profusion of his reddish-brown hair, to his finely shaped sensitive lips, but for two marked peculiarities in him which would have shown me to be wrong – that is to say: the expression of power about his head, and the signs of masculine resolution presented by his mouth and chin.

On entering the room, the first person, and the only person, who attracted his attention was Cristel.

He bowed, smiled, possessed himself abruptly of her hand, and kissed it. She tried to withdraw it from his grasp, and met with an obstinate resistance. His gallantry addressed her in sweet words; and his voice destroyed their charm by the dreary monotony of the tone in which he spoke. 'On this lovely day, Cristel, Nature pleads for me. Your heart feels the sunshine and softens towards the poor deaf man who worships you. Ah, my dear, it's useless to say No. My affliction is my happiness, when you say cruel things to me. I live in my fool's paradise; I don't hear you.' He tried to draw her nearer to him. 'Come, my angel; let me kiss you.'

She made a second attempt to release herself; and this time, she wrenched her hand out of his grasp with a strength for which he was not prepared.

That fiercest anger which turns the face pale, was the anger that had possession of Cristel as she took refuge with her father. 'You asked me to bear with that man,' she said, 'because he paid you a good rent. I tell you this, father; my patience is coming to an end. Either he must go, or I must go. Make up your mind to choose between your money and me.'

Old Toller astonished me. He seemed to have caught the infection of his daughter's anger. Placed between Cristel and his money, he really acted as if he preferred Cristel. He hobbled up to his lodger, and shook his infirm fists, and screamed at the highest pitch of his old cracked voice: 'Let her be, or I won't have you here no longer! You deaf adder, let her be!'

The sensitive nerves of the deaf man shrank as those shrill tones pierced them. 'If you want to speak to me, write it!' he

said, with rage and suffering in every line of his face. He tore
from his pocket his little book, filled with blank leaves, and
threw it at Toller's head. 'Write,' he repeated. 'If you murder
me with your screeching again, look out for your skinny
throat – I'll throttle you.'

Cristel picked up the book. She was gratefully sensible of
her father's interference. 'He shall know what you said to
him,' she promised the old man. 'I'll write it myself.'

She took the pencil from its sheath in the leather binding of
the book. Controlling himself, the lover whom she hated
advanced towards her with a persuasive smile.

'Have you forgiven me?' he asked. 'Have you been speaking
kindly of me? I think I see it in your face. There are some deaf
people who can tell what is said by looking at the speaker's
lips. I am too stupid, or too impatient, or too wicked to be
able to do that. Write it for me, dear, and make me happy for
the day.'

Cristel was not attending to him, she was speaking to me. 'I
hope, sir, you don't think that father and I are to blame for
what has happened this morning,' she said. He looked where
she was looking – and discovered, for the first time, that I was
in the room.

He had alluded to his wickedness a moment since. When his
face turned my way, I thought it bore witness to his
knowledge of his own character.

'Why didn't you come to my side of the house?' he said to
me. 'What am I to understand, sir, by seeing you here?'

Cristel dropped her book on the table, and hurried to me in
breathless surprise. 'He speaks as if he knew you!' she cried.
'What does it mean?'

'Only that I met him last night,' I explained, 'after leaving
you.'

'Did you know him before that?'

'No. He was a perfect stranger to me.'

He picked up his book from the table, and took his pencil
out of Cristel's hand, while we were speaking. 'I want my
answer,' he said, handing me the book and the pencil. I gave
him his answer.

'You find me here, because I don't wish to return to your
side of the house.'

'Is that the impression,' he asked, 'produced by what I allowed you to read?'

I replied by a sign in the affirmative. He inquired next if I had brought his portfolio with me. I put it at once into his hand.

In some way unknown to me, I had apparently roused his suspicions. He opened the portfolio, and counted the loose leaves of writing in it carefully. While he was absorbed in this occupation, old Toller's eccentricity assumed a new form. His little restless black eyes followed the movements of his lodger's fingers, as they turned over leaf after leaf of the manuscript, with such eager curiosity and interest that I looked at him in surprise. Finding that he had attracted my notice, he showed no signs of embarrassment – he seized the opportunity of asking for information.

'Did my gentleman trust you, sir, with all that writing?' he began.

'Yes.'

'Did he want you to read it?'

'He did.'

'What's it all about, sir?'

Confronted by this cool inquiry, I informed Mr Toller that the demands of curiosity had their limits, and that he had reached them. On this ground, I declined to answer any more questions. Mr Toller went on with his questions immediately.

'Do you notice, sir, that he seems to set a deal of store by his writings? Perhaps you can say what the value of them may be?'

I shook my head. 'It won't do, Mr Toller!'

He tried again – I declare it positively, he tried again. 'You'll excuse me, sir? I've never seen his portfolio before. Am I right if I think you know where he keeps it?'

'Spare your breath, Mr Toller. Once more, it won't do!'

Cristel joined us, amazed at his pertinacity. 'Why are you so anxious, father, to know about that portfolio?' she asked.

Her father seemed to have reasons of his own for following my example, and declining to answer questions. More polite, however, than I had been, he left his resolution to be inferred. His daughter was answered by a few general remarks, setting forth the advantage to the landlord of having a lodger who had lost one of his senses.

'You see there's something convenient, my dear, in the circumstance of that nice-looking gentleman over there being deaf. We can talk about him before his face, just as comfortably as if it was behind his back. Isn't that so, Mr Gerard? Don't you see it yourself, Cristy? For instance, I say it without fear in his presence: 'tis the act of a fool to be fumbling over writings, when there's nothing in them that's not well known to himself already – unless indeed they are worth money, which I don't doubt is no secret to *you*, Mr Gerard? Eh? I beg your pardon, sir, did you speak? No? I beg your pardon again. Yes, yes, Cristy, I'm noticing him; he's done with his writings. Suppose I offer to put them away for him? You can see in his face he finds the tale of them correct. He's coming this way. What's he going to do next?'

He was going to establish a claim on my gratitude, by relieving me of Giles Toller.

'I have something to say to Mr Roylake,' he announced, with a haughty look at his landlord. 'Mind! I don't forget your screaming at me just now, and I intend to know what you meant by it. That will do. Get out of the way.'

The old fellow received his dismissal with a low bow, and left the kitchen with a look at The Lodger which revealed (unless I was entirely mistaken) a sly sense of triumph. What did it mean?

The deaf man addressed me with a cold and distant manner. 'We must understand each other,' he said. 'Will you follow me to my side of the cottage?' I shook my head. 'Very well,' he resumed; 'we will have it out, here. When I trusted you with my confession last night, I left you to decide (after reading it) whether you would make an enemy of me or not. You remember that?' I nodded my head. 'Then I now ask you, Mr Roylake: Which are we – enemies or friends?'

I took the pencil, and wrote my reply:

'Neither enemies nor friends. We are strangers from this time forth.'

Some internal struggle produced a change in his face – visible for one moment, hidden from me in a moment more. 'I think you will regret the decision at which you have arrived.' He said that, and saluted me with his grandly gracious bow. As he turned away, he perceived Cristel at the other end of the room, and eagerly joined her.

'The only happy moments I have are my moments passed in your presence,' he said. 'I shall trouble you no more for to-day. Give me a little comfort to take back with me to my solitude. I didn't notice that there were other persons present when I asked leave to kiss you. May I hope that you forgive me?'

He held out his hand; it was not taken. He waited a little, in the vain hope that she would relent: she turned away from him.

A spasm of pain distorted his handsome face. He opened the door that led to his side of the cottage – paused – and looked back at Cristel. She took no notice of him. As he moved again to the door and left us, the hysterical passion in him forced its way outward – he burst into tears.

The dog sprang up from his refuge under the table, and shook himself joyfully. Cristel breathed again freely, and joined me at my end of the room. Shall I make another acknowledgment of weakness? I began to fear that we might all of us (even including the dog!) have been a little hard on the poor deaf wretch who had gone away in such bitter distress. I communicated this view of the matter to Cristel. She failed to see it as I did.

The dog laid his head on her lap, asking to be caressed. She patted him while she answered me.

'I agree with this old friend, Mr Gerard. We were both of us frightened, on the very first day, when the person you are pitying came to lodge with us. I have got to hate him, since that time – perhaps to despise him. But the dog has never changed; he feels and knows there is something dreadful in that man. One of these days, poor Ponto may turn out to be right. – May I ask you something, sir?'

'Of course!'

'You won't think I am presuming on your kindness?'

'You ought to know me better than that, Cristel!'

'The truth is, sir, I have been a little startled by what I saw in our Lodger's face, when he asked if you were his enemy or his friend. I know he is thought to be handsome – but, Mr Gerard, those beautiful eyes of his sometimes tell tales; and I have seen his pretty complexion change to a colour that turned him into an ugly man. Will you tell me what you wrote when you answered him?'

I repeated what I had written, word for word. It failed to satisfy her.

'He is very vain,' she said, 'and you may have wounded his vanity by treating him like a stranger, after he had given you his writings to read, and invited you to his room. But I thought I saw something much worse than mortification in his face. Shall I be taking a liberty, if I ask how it was you got acquainted with him last night?'

She was evidently in earnest. I saw that I must answer her without reserve; and I was a little afraid of being myself open to a suspicion of vanity, if I mentioned the distrust which I had innocently excited in the mind of my new acquaintance. In this state of embarrassment I took a young man's way out of the difficulty, and spoke lightly of a serious thing.

'I became acquainted with your deaf Lodger, Cristel, under ridiculous circumstances. He saw us talking last night, and did me the honour to be jealous of me.'

I had expected to see her blush. To my surprise she turned pale, and vehemently remonstrated.

'Don't laugh, sir! There's nothing to be amused at in what you have just told me. You didn't go into his room last night? Oh, what made you do that!'

I described his successful appeal to my compassion – not very willingly, for it made me look (as I thought) like a weak person. Little by little, she extracted from me the rest: how he objected to find a young man, especially in my social position, talking to Cristel; how he insisted on my respecting his claims, and engaging not to see her again; how, when I refused to do this, he gave me his confession to read, so that I might find out what a formidable man I was setting at defiance; how I had not been in the least alarmed, and had treated him (as Cristel had just heard) on the footing of a perfect stranger.

'There's the whole story,' I concluded. 'Like a scene in a play, isn't it?'

She protested once more against the light tone that I persisted in assuming.

I tell you again, sir, this is no laughing matter. You have roused his jealousy. You had better have roused the fury of a wild beast. Knowing what you know of him, why did you stay here, when he came in? And, oh, why did I humiliate him in your presence? Leave us, Mr Gerard – pray, pray leave us, and don't come near this place again till father has got rid of him.'

Did she think I was to be so easily frightened as that? My sense of my own importance was up in arms at the bare suspicion of it!

'My dear child,' I said grandly, 'do you really suppose I am afraid of that poor wretch? Am I to give up the pleasure of seeing you, because a mad fellow is simple enough to think you will marry him? Absurd, Cristel – absurd!'

The poor girl wrung her hands in despair.

'Oh, sir, don't distress me by talking in that way! Do please remember who you are, and who I am. If I was the miserable means of your coming to any harm – I can't bear even to speak of it! Pray don't think me bold; I don't know how to express myself. You ought never to have come here; you ought to go; you *must* go!'

Driven by strong impulse, she ran to the place in which I had left my hat, and brought it to me, and opened the door with a look of entreaty which it was impossible to resist. It would have been an act of downright cruelty to persist in opposing her. 'I wouldn't distress you, Cristel, for the whole world,' I said – and left her to conclude that I had felt the influence of her entreaties in the right way. She tried to thank me; the tears rose in her eyes – she signed to me to leave her, poor soul, as if she felt ashamed of herself. I was shocked; I was grieved; I was more than ever secretly resolved to go back to her. When we said good-bye – I have been told that I did wrong; I meant no harm – I kissed her.

Having traversed the short distance between the cottage and the wood, I remembered that I had left my walking-stick behind me, and returned to get it.

Cristel was leaving the kitchen; I saw her at the door which communicated with the Lodger's side of the cottage. Her back was turned towards me; astonishment held me silent. She opened the door, passed through it, and closed it behind her.

Going to that man, after she had repelled his advances, in my presence! Going to the enemy against whom she had warned me, after I had first been persuaded to leave her! Angry thoughts these – and surely thoughts unworthy of me? If it had been the case of another man, I should have said he was jealous. Jealous of the miller's daughter – in my position? Absurd! contemptible! But I was still in such a vile temper that

I determined to let Cristel know she had been discovered. Taking one of my visiting cards, I wrote on it: 'I came back for my stick, and saw you go to him.' After I had pinned this spiteful little message to the door, so that she might see it when she returned, I suffered a disappointment. I was not half so well satisfied with myself as I had anticipated.

CHAPTER VII

THE BEST SOCIETY

Leaving the cottage for the second time, I was met at the door by a fat man of solemn appearance dressed in black, who respectfully touched his hat. My angry humour acknowledged the harmless stranger's salute by a rude inquiry: 'What the devil do you want?' Instead of resenting this uncivil language, he indirectly reproved me by becoming more respectful than ever.

'My mistress desires me to tell you, sir, that luncheon is waiting.'

I was in the presence of a thoroughbred English servant – and I had failed to discover it until he spoke of his mistress! I had also, by keeping luncheon waiting, treated an English institution with contempt. And, worse even than this, as a misfortune which personally affected me, my stepmother evidently knew that I had paid another visit to the mill.

I hurried along the woodland path, followed by the fat domestic in black. Not used apparently to force his legs into rapid motion, he articulated with the greatest difficulty in answering my next question: 'How did you know where to find me?'

'Mrs Roylake ordered inquiries to be made, sir. The head gardener——' There his small reserves of breath failed him.

'The head gardener saw me?'

'Yes, sir.'

'When?'

'Hours ago, sir – when you went into Toller's cottage.'

I troubled my fat friend with no more questions.

Returning to the house, and making polite apologies, I discovered one more among Mrs Roylake's many accomplishments. She possessed two smiles – a sugary smile

46

(with which I was already acquainted), and an acid smile which she apparently reserved for special occasions. It made its appearance when I led her to the luncheon table.

'Don't let me detain you,' my stepmother began.

'Won't you give me some luncheon?' I inquired.

'Dear me! hav'n't you lunched already?'

'Where should I lunch, my dear lady?' I thought this would induce the sugary smile to show itself. I was wrong.

'Where?' Mrs Roylake repeated. 'With your friends at the mill, of course. Very inhospitable not to offer you lunch. When are we to have flour cheaper?'

I began to get sulky. All I said was: 'I don't know.'

'Curious!' Mrs Roylake observed. 'You not only don't get luncheon among your friends: you don't even get information. To know a miller, and not to know the price of flour, is ignorance presented in one of its most pitiable aspects. And how is Miss Toller looking? Perfectly charming?'

I was angry by this time. 'You have exactly described her,' I said.

Mrs Roylake began to get angry, on her side.

'Surely a little coarse and vulgar?' she suggested, reverting to poor Cristel.

'Would you like to judge for yourself?' I asked. 'I shall be happy, Mrs Roylake to take you to the mill.'

My stepmother's knowledge of the world implied considerable acquaintance – how obtained I do not pretend to know – with the characters of men. Discovering that she was in danger of over-stepping the limits of my patience, she drew back with a skill which performed the retrograde movement without permitting it to betray itself.

'We have carried our little joke, my dear Gerard, far enough,' she said. 'I fancy your residence in Germany has rather blunted your native English sense of humour. You don't suppose, I hope and trust, that I am so insensible to our relative positions as to think of interfering in your choice of friends or associates. If you are not aware of it already, let me remind you that this house is now yours; not mine. I live here – gladly live here, my dear boy – by your indulgence; fortified (I am sure) by your regard for your excellent father's wishes as expressed in his will——'

I stopped her there. She had got the better of me with a dexterity which I see now, but which I was not clever enough to appreciate at the time. In a burst of generosity, I entreated her to consider Trimley Deen as her house, and never to mention such a shocking subject as my authority again.

After this, need I say that the most amiable of women took me out in her carriage, and introduced me to some of the best society in England?

If I could only remember all the new friends to whom I made my bow, as well as the conversation in which we indulged, I might write a few pages here, interesting in a high degree to persons with well-balanced minds. Unhappily, so far as my own impressions were concerned, the best society proved to be always the same society. Every house that we entered was in the same beautiful order; every mistress of the house was dressed in the best taste; every master of the house had the same sensible remarks to make on conservative prospects at the coming election; every young gentleman wanted to know how my game preserves had been looked after in my absence; every young lady said: 'How nice it must have been, Mr Roylake, to find yourself again at Trimley Deen.' Has anybody ever suffered as I suffered, during that round of visits, under the desire to yawn and the effort to suppress it? Is there any sympathetic soul who can understand me, when I say that I would have given a hundred pounds for a gag, and for the privilege of using it to stop my stepmother's pleasant chat in the carriage, following on our friends' pleasant chat in the drawing-room? Finally, when we got home, and when Mrs Roylake kindly promised me another round of visits, and more charming people in the neighbourhood to see, will any good Christian forgive me, if I own that I took advantage of being alone to damn the neighbourhood, and to feel relieved by it?

Now that I was no longer obliged to listen to polite strangers, my thoughts reverted to Cristel, and to the suspicions that she had roused in me.

Recovering its influence, in the interval that had passed, my better nature sharply reproached me. I had presumed to blame Cristel, with nothing to justify me but my own perverted view of her motives. How did I know that she had not opened that door, and gone to that side of the cottage, with a perfectly harmless object in view? I was really anxious, if I could find the right way to do it, to make amends for an act of injustice of which I felt ashamed. If I am asked why I was as eager to set myself right with a miller's daughter, as if she had been a young lady in the higher ranks of life, I can only reply that no such view of our relative positions as this ever occurred to me. A strange state of mind, no doubt. What was the right explanation of it?

The right explanation presented itself at a later time, when troubles had quickened my intellect, and when I could estimate the powerful influence of circumstances at its true value.

I had returned to England, to fill a prominent place in my own little world, without relations whom I loved, without friends whose society I could enjoy. Hopeful, ardent, eager for the enjoyment of life, I had brought with me to my own country the social habits and the free range of thought of a foreign University; and, as a matter of course, I failed to feel any sympathy with the society – new to me – in which my lot had been cast. Beset by these disadvantages, I had met with a girl, possessed of remarkable personal attractions, and associated with my earliest remembrances of my own happy life and of my mother's kindness – a girl, at once simple and spirited; unspoilt by the world and the world's ways, and placed in a position of peril due to the power of her own beauty, which added to the interest that she naturally inspired. Estimating these circumstances at their true value, did a state of mind which rendered me insensible to the distinctions that separate the classes in England, stand in any need of explanation? As I thought – and think still – it explained itself.

My stepmother and I parted on the garden terrace, which ran along the pleasant southern side of the house.

The habits that I had contracted, among my student friends in Germany, made tobacco and beer necessary accompaniments to the process of thinking. I had nearly exhausted my cigar, my jug, and my thoughts, when I saw two men approaching me from the end of the terrace.

As they came nearer, I recognized in one of the men my fat domestic in black. He stopped the person who was accompanying him, and came on to me by himself.

'Will you see that man, sir, waiting behind me?'

'Who is he?'

'I don't know, sir. He says he has got a letter to give you, and he must put it in your own hands. I think myself he's a beggar. He's excessively insolent – he insists on seeing you. Shall I tell him to go?'

The servant evidently expected me to say Yes. He was disappointed; my curiosity was roused; I said I would see the insolent stranger.

As he approached me, the man certainly did not look like a beggar. Poor he might be, judging by his dress. The upper part of him was clothed in an old shooting jacket of velveteen; his legs presented a pair of trousers, once black, now turning brown with age. Both garments were too long for him, and both were kept scrupulously clean. He was a short man, thickly and strongly made. Impenetrable composure appeared on his ugly face. His eyes were sunk deep in his head; his nose had evidently been broken and not successfully mended; his grey hair, when he took off his hat on addressing me, was cut short, and showed his low forehead and his bull neck. An Englishman of the last generation would, as I have since been informed, have set him down as a retired prize-fighter. Thanks to my ignorance of the pugilistic glories of my native country, I was totally at a loss what to make of him.

'Have I the honour of speaking to Mr Roylake?' he asked.

His quiet steady manner prepossessed me in his favour; it showed no servile reverence for the accident of birth, on the one hand, and no insolent assertion of independence, on the other. When I had told him that my name was Roylake, he searched one of the large pockets of his shooting jacket, produced a letter, and silently offered it to me.

Before I took the letter – seeing that he was a stranger, and that he mentioned no name known to me – I thought it desirable to make some inquiry.

'Is it a letter of your own writing?' I asked.

'No, sir.'

'Who sends you with it?'

He was apparently a man of few words. 'My master,' was the guarded answer that this odd servant returned.

I became as inquisitive as old Toller himself.

'Who is your master?' I went on.

The reply staggered me. Speaking as quietly and respectfully as ever, he said: 'I can't tell you, sir.'

'Do you mean that you are forbidden to tell me?'

'No, sir.'

'Then what do you mean?'

'I mean that I don't know my master's name.'

I instantly took the letter from him, and looked at the address. For once in a way, I had jumped at a conclusion and I had proved to be right. The handwriting on the letter, and the handwriting of the confession which I had read overnight, were one and the same.

'Are you to wait for an answer?' I asked, as I opened the envelope.

'I am to wait, sir, if you tell me to do so.'

The letter was a long one. After running my eye over the first sentences, I surprised myself by acting discreetly. 'You needn't wait,' I said; 'I will send a reply.' The man of few words raised his shabby hat, turned about in silence, and left me.

CHAPTER VIII

THE DEAF LODGER

The letter was superscribed: 'Private and Confidential.' It was written in these words:

Sir, – You will do me grievous wrong if you suppose that I am trying to force myself on your acquaintance. My object in writing is to prevent you (if I can) from misinterpreting my language and my conduct, on the only two occasions when we happen to have met.

I am conscious that you must have thought me rude and ungrateful – perhaps even a little mad – when I returned your kindness last night, in honouring me with a visit, by using language which has justified you in treating me as a stranger.

Fortunately for myself, I gave you my autobiography to read. After what you now know of me, I may hope that your sense of justice will make some allowance for a man, tried (I had almost written, cursed) by such suffering as mine.

There are other deaf persons, as I have heard, who set me a good example.

They feel the consolations of religion. Their sweet tempers find relief even under the loss of the most precious of all the senses. They mix with society; submitting to their dreadful isolation, and preserving unimpaired sympathy with their happier fellow-creatures who can hear. I am not one of those persons. With sorrow I say it – I never have submitted, I never can submit, to my hard fate.

Let me not omit to ask your indulgence for my behaviour, when we met at the cottage this morning.

What unfortunate impression I may have produced on you, I dare not inquire. So little capable am I of concealing the vile feelings which sometimes get the better of me, that Miss Cristel (observe that I mention her with respect) appears to have felt positive alarm, on your account, when she looked at me.

I may tell you, in confidence, that this charming person came to my side of the cottage, as soon as you had taken your departure, to intercede with me in your favour. "If your wicked mind is planning to do evil to Mr Roylake," she wrote in my book, "either you will promise me to give it up, or I will never allow you to see me again; I will even leave home secretly, to be out of your way." In that strong language she expressed – how shall I refer to it? – shall I say the sisterly interest that she felt in your welfare?

I laid down the letter for a moment. If I had not already reproached myself for having misjudged Cristel – and if I had not, in that way, done her some little justice in my own better thoughts – I should never have recovered my self-respect after reading the deaf man's letter. The good girl! The dear good girl! Yes: that was how I thought of her, under the windows of my stepmother's boudoir – while Mrs Roylake, for all I knew to the contrary, might be looking down at me, and when Lady Lena, the noble and beautiful was coming to dinner!

The letter concluded as follows:

To return to myself. I gave Miss Cristel the promise on which she insisted; and then, naturally enough, I inquired into her motive for interfering in your favour.

She frankly admitted that she was interested in you. First: in grateful remembrance of old times, when you and your mother had been always good to her. Secondly: because she had found you as kind and as friendly as ever, now that you were a man and had become the greatest landowner in the county. There was the explanation I had asked for, at my service. And, on that, she left me.

Did I believe her when I was meditating on our interview, alone in my room? Or did I suspect you of having robbed me of the only consolation that makes my life endurable?

No such unworthy suspicion as this was admitted to my mind. With all my heart, I believe her. And with perfect sincerity, I trust You.

If your knowledge of me has failed to convince you that there is any such thing as a better side to my nature, you will no doubt conclude that this letter is a trick of mine to throw you off your guard; and you will continue to distrust me as obstinately as ever. In that case, I will merely remind you that my letter is private and confidential, and I will not ask you to send me a reply.

I remain, Sir, yours as you may receive me,

THE DEAF LODGER.

I wonder what another man, in my position, would have done when he had read this letter? Would he have seen in it nothing to justify some respect and some kindly feeling towards the writer? Could he have reconciled it to his conscience to leave the afflicted man who had trusted him without a word of reply?

For my part (do not forget what a young man I was in those days), I made up my mind to reply in the friendliest manner – that is to say, in person.

After consulting my watch, I satisfied myself that I could go to the mill, and get back again, before the hour fixed for our late dinner – supper we should have called it in Germany. For the second time that day, and without any hesitation, I took the road that led to Fordwitch Wood.

Crossing the glade, I encountered a stout young woman, filling a can with water from the spring. She curtseyed on seeing me. I asked if she belonged to the village.

The reply informed me that I had taken another of my servants for a stranger. The stout nymph of the spring was my kitchen-maid; and she was fetching the water which we drank at the house; 'and there's no water, sir, like *yours* for all the country round.' Furnished with these stores of information, I went my way, and the kitchen-maid went hers. She spoke, of course, of having seen her new master, on returning to the servants' hall. In this manner, as I afterwards heard, the discovery of me at the spring, and my departure by the path that led to the mill, reached Mrs Roylake's ears – the medium of information being the lady's own maid. So far, Fordwitch Wood seemed to be a place to avoid, in the interests of my domestic tranquillity.

Arriving at the cottage, I found The Lodger standing by the open window at which I had first seen him.

But, on this occasion, his personal appearance had undergone a singular process of transformation. The lower part of his face, from his nostrils to his chin, was hidden by a white handkerchief tied round it. He had removed the stopper from a strangely shaped bottle, and was absorbed in watching some interesting condition in a dusky liquid that it contained. To attract his attention by speaking was of course out of the question; I could only wait until he happened to look my way.

My patience was not severely tried: he soon replaced the stopper in the bottle, and, looking up from it, saw me. With his free hand, he quickly removed the handkerchief, and spoke.

'Let me ask you to wait in the boat-house,' he said; 'I will come to you directly.' He pointed round the corner of the new cottage; indicating of course the side of it that was farthest from the old building.

Following his directions, I first passed the door that he used in leaving or returning to his room, and then gained the bank of the river. On my right hand rose the mill building, with its big water-wheel – and, above it, a little higher up the stream, I recognized the boat-house; built out in the water on piles, and approached by a wooden pier.

No structure of this elaborate and expensive sort would have been set up by my father, for the miller's convenience. The boat-house had been built, many years since, by a rich retired tradesman with a mania for aquatic pursuits. Our ugly river had not answered his expectations, and our neighbourhood had abstained from returning his visits. When he left us, with his wherries and canoes and outriggers, the miller took possession of the abandoned boat-house. 'It's the sort of fixture that you don't pay nohow,' old Toller remarked. 'Suppose you remove it – there's a waste of money. Suppose you knock it to pieces – is it worth a rich gentleman's while to sell a cartload of firewood?' Neither of these alternatives having been adopted, and nobody wanting an empty boat-house, the clumsy mill boat, hitherto tied to a stake, and exposed to the worst that the weather could do to injure it, was now snugly sheltered under a roof; with empty lockers (once occupied by aquatic luxuries) gaping on either side of it.

I was looking out on the river, and thinking of all that had happened since my first meeting with Cristel by moonlight, when the voice of the deaf man made itself discordantly heard, behind me.

'Let me apologize for receiving you here,' he said; 'and let me trouble you with one more of my confessions. Like other unfortunate deaf people, I suffer from nervous irritability. Sometimes, we restlessly change our places of abode. And sometimes, as in my case, we take refuge in variety of occupation. You remember the ideal narratives of crime which I was so fond of writing at one time?'

I gave the affirmative answer, in the usual way.

'Well,' he went on, 'my literary inventions have ceased to interest me. I have latterly resumed the chemical studies, associated with that happy time in my life when I was entering on the medical profession. Unluckily for you, I have been trying an experiment to-day, which makes such an abominable smell in my room that I dare not ask you to enter it. The fumes are not only disagreeable, but in some degree dangerous. You saw me at the window, perhaps, with my nose and mouth protected before I opened the bottle?'

I repeated the affirmative sign. He produced his little book of blank leaves, and opened it ready for use.

'May I hope,' he said, 'that your visit is intended as a favourable reply to my letter?'

I took the pencil, and answered him in these terms:

'Your letter has satisfied me that I was mistaken in treating you like a stranger. I have come here to express my regret at having failed to do you justice. Pray be assured that I believe in your better nature, and that I accept your letter in the spirit in which you have written it.'

He read my reply, and suddenly looked at me.

Never had I seen his beautiful eyes so brightly soft, so irresistibly tender, as they appeared now. He held out his hand to me. It is one of my small merits to be (in the popular phrase) as good as my word. I took his hand; well knowing that the action committed me to accepting his friendship.

In relating the events which form this narrative, I look back at the chain, as I add to it link by link – sometimes with surprise, sometimes with interest, and sometimes with the discovery that I have omitted a circumstance which it is necessary to replace. But I search my memory in vain, while I dwell on the lines that I have just written, for a recollection of some attendant event which might have warned me of the peril towards which I was advancing blindfold. My remembrance presents us as standing together with clasped hands; but nothing in the slightest degree ominous is associated with the picture. There was no sinister chill communicated from his hand to mine; no shocking accident happened close by us in the river; not even a passing cloud obscured the sunlight, shining in its gayest glory over our heads.

After having shaken hands, neither he nor I had apparently anything more to say. A little embarrassed, I turned to the boat-house window, and looked out. Trifling as the action was, my companion noticed it.

'Do you like that muddy river?' he asked.

I took the pencil again: 'Old associations make even the ugly Loke interesting to me.'

He sighed as he read those words. 'I wish, Mr Roylake, I could say the same. Your interesting river frightens me.'

It was needless to ask for the pencil again. My puzzled face begged for an explanation.

'When you were in my room,' he said, 'you may have noticed a second window which looks out on The Loke. I have got into a bad habit of sitting by that window on moonlight nights. I watch the flow of the stream, and it seems to associate itself with the flow of my thoughts. Nothing remarkable, so far – while I am awake. But, later, when I get to sleep, dreams come to me. All of them, sir, without exception connect Cristel with the river. Look at the stealthy current that makes no sound. In my last night's sleep, it made itself heard; it was flowing in my ears with a water-music of its own. No longer

my deaf ears; I heard, in my dream, as well as you can hear.
Yes; the same water-music, singing over and over again the
same horrid song: "Fool, fool, no Cristel for you; bid her
good-bye, bid her good-bye." I saw her floating away from
me on those hideous waters. The cruel current held me back
when I tried to follow her. I struggled and screamed and
shivered and cried. I woke up with a start that shook me to
pieces, and cursed your interesting river. Don't write to me
about it again. Don't look at it again. Why did you bring up
the subject? I beg your pardon; I had no right to say that. Let
me be polite; let me be hospitable. I beg to invite you to come
and see me, when my room is purified from its pestilent smell.
I can only offer you a cup of tea. Oh, that river, that river,
what devil set me talking about it? I'm not mad, Mr Roylake;
only wretched. When may I expect you? Choose your own
evening next week.'

Who could help pitying him? Compared with my sound
sweet dreamless sleep, what dreadful nights were his!

I accepted his invitation as a matter of course. When we had
completed our arrangements, it was time for me to think of
returning to Trimley Deen. Moving towards the door, I
accidentally directed his attention to the pier by which the
boat-house was approached.

His face instantly reminded me of Cristel's description of
him, when he was strongly and evilly moved. I too saw 'his
beautiful eyes tell tales, and his pretty complexion change to a
colour which turned him into an ugly man.' He seized my
arm, and pointed to the pier, at the end of it which joined the
river-bank. 'Pray accept my excuses; I can't answer for my
temper if that wretch comes near me.' With this apology he
hurried away; and sly Giles Toller, having patiently waited
until the coast was clear, accosted me with his best bow, and
said: 'Beautiful weather, isn't it, sir?'

I had no remarks to make on the weather; but I was
interested in discovering what had happened at the cottage.

'You have mortally offended the gentleman who has just
left me,' I said. 'What have you done?'

Mr Toller had purposes of his own to serve, and kept those
purposes (as usual) exclusively in view: *he* presented deaf ears
to me now!

'I don't think I ever remember such wonderful weather, sir, in my time; and I'm an old fellow, as I needn't tell you. Being at the mill just now, I saw you in the boat-house, and came to pay my respects. Would you be so good as to look at this slip of paper, Mr Gerard? If you will kindly ask what it is, you will in a manner help me.'

I knew but too well what it was. 'The repairs again!' I said resignedly. 'Hand it over, you obstinate old man.'

Mr Toller was so tickled by my discovery, and by the cheering prospect consequent on seeing his list of repairs safe in my pocket, that he laughed until I really thought he would shake his lean little body to pieces. By way of bringing his merriment to an end, I assumed a look of severity, and insisted on knowing how he had offended The Lodger. My venerable tenant, trembling for his repairs, drifted into a question of personal experience, and seemed to anticipate that it might improve my temper.

'When you have a woman about the house, Mr Gerard, you may have noticed that she's an everlasting expense to you – especially when she's a young one. Isn't that so?'

I inquired if he applied this remark to his daughter.

'That's it, sir; I'm talking of Cristy. When her back's up, there isn't her equal in England for strong language. My gentleman has misbehaved himself in some way (since you were with us this morning, sir); how, I don't quite understand. All I can tell you is, I've given him notice to quit. A clear loss of money to me every week, and Cristy's responsible for it. Yes, sir! I've been worked up to it by my girl. If Cristy's mother had asked me to get rid of a paying lodger, I should have told her to go to —— we won't say where, sir; you'll know where when you're married yourself. The upshot of it is that I have offended my gentleman, for the sake of my girl: which last is a luxury I can't afford, unless I let the rooms again. If you hear of a tenant, say what a good landlord I am, and what sweet pretty rooms I've got to let.'

I led the way to the bank of the river, before Mr Toller could make any more requests.

We passed the side of the old cottage. The door was open; and I saw Cristel employed in the kitchen.

My watch told me that I had still two or three minutes to spare; and my guilty remembrance of the message that I had pinned to the door suggested an immediate expression of regret. I approached Cristel with a petition for pardon on my lips. She looked distrustfully at the door of communication with the new cottage, as if she expected to see it opened from the other side.

'Not now!' she said – and went on sadly with her household work.

'May I see you to-morrow?' I asked.

'It had better not be here, sir,' was the only reply she made.

I offered to meet her at any other place which she might appoint. Cristel persisted in leaving it to me; she spoke absently, as if she was thinking all the time of something else. I could propose no better place, at the moment, than the spring in Fordwitch Wood. She consented to meet me there, on the next day, if seven o'clock in the morning would not be too early for me. My German habits had accustomed me to early rising. She heard me tell her this – and looked again at The Lodger's door – and abruptly wished me good evening.

Her polite father was shocked at this unceremonious method of dismissing the great man, who had only to say the word and stop the repairs. 'Where are your manners, Cristy?' he asked indignantly. Before he could say another word, I was out of the cottage.

As I passed the spring on my way home, I thought of my two appointments. On that evening, my meeting with the daughter of the lord. On the next morning, my meeting with the daughter of the miller. Lady Lena at dinner; Cristel before breakfast. If Mrs Roylake found out *that* social contrast, what would she say? I was a merry young fool; I burst out laughing.

CHAPTER IX

MRS ROYLAKE'S GAME: FIRST MOVE

The dinner at Trimley Deen has left in my memory little that I can distinctly recall. Only a faintly-marked vision of Lady Lena rewards me for doing my best to remember her. A tall slim graceful person, dressed in white with a simplicity which is the perfection of art, presents to my admiration gentle blue eyes, a pale complexion delicately touched with colour, a well-carried head crowned by lovely light brown hair. So far, time helps the reviving past to come to life again – and permits nothing more. I cannot say that I now remember the voice once so musical in my ears, or that I am able to repeat the easy unaffected talk which once interested me, or that I see again (in my thoughts) the perfect charm of manner which delighted everybody, not forgetting myself. My unworthy self, I might say; for I was the only young man, honoured by an introduction to Lady Lena, who stopped at admiration, and never made use of opportunity to approach love.

On the other hand, I distinctly recollect what my stepmother and I said to each other when our guests had wished us good-night.

If I am asked to account for this, I can only reply that the conspiracy to lead me into proposing marriage to Lady Lena first showed itself on the occasion to which I have referred. In her eagerness to reach her ends, Mrs Roylake failed to handle the fine weapons of deception as cleverly as usual. Even I, with my small experience of worldly women, discovered the object that she had in view.

I had retired to the seclusion of the smoking-room, and was already encircled by the clouds which float on the heaven of tobacco, when I heard a rustling of silk outside, and saw the smile of Mrs Roylake beginning to captivate me through the open door.

61

'If you throw away your cigar,' cried this amiable person, 'you will drive me out of the room. Dear Gerard, I like your smoke.'

My fat man in black, coming in at the moment to bring me some soda water, looked at his mistress with an expression of amazement and horror, which told me that he now saw Mrs Roylake in the smoking-room for the first time. I involved myself in new clouds. If I suffocated my stepmother, her own polite equivocation would justify the act. She settled herself opposite to me in an armchair. The agonies that she must have suffered, in preventing her face from expressing emotions of disgust, I dare not attempt to imagine, even at this distance of time.

'Now, Gerard, let us talk about the two ladies. What do you think of my friend, Lady Rachel?'

'I don't like your friend, Lady Rachel.'

'You astonish me. Why?'

'I think she's a false woman.'

'Heavens, what a thing to say of a lady – and that lady my friend! Her politics may very reasonably have surprised you. But surely her vigorous intellect ought to have challenged your admiration; you can't deny that?'

I was not clever enough to be able to deny it. But I was bold enough to say that Lady Rachel seemed to me to be a woman who talked for the sake of producing effect. She expressed opinions, as I ventured to declare, which (in her position) I did not believe she could honestly entertain.

Mrs Roylake entered a vigorous protest. She assured me that I was completely mistaken. 'Lady Rachel,' she said, 'is the most perfectly candid person in the whole circle of my acquaintance.'

With the best intentions on my part, this was more than I could patiently endure.

'Isn't she the daughter of a nobleman?' I asked. 'Doesn't she owe her rank and her splendour, and the respect that people show to her, to the fortunate circumstance of her birth? And yet she talks as if she was a red republican. You yourself heard her say that she was a thorough Radical, and hoped she might live to see the House of Lords abolished. Oh, I heard her! And what is more, I listened so attentively to such sentiments as these, from a lady with a title, that I can repeat, word for word, what she said next. "We hav'n't deserved our own titles; we hav'n't earned our own incomes; and we legislate for the country, without having been trusted by the country. In short, we are a set of impostors, and the time is coming when we shall be found out." Do you believe she really meant that? All as false as false can be – that's what I say of it.'

There I stopped, privately admiring my own eloquence.

Quite a mistake on my part; my eloquence had done just what Mrs Roylake wished me to do. She wanted an opportunity of dropping Lady Rachel, and taking up Lady Lena, with a producible reason which forbade the imputation of a personal motive on her part. I had furnished her with the reason. Thus far, I cannot deny it, my stepmother was equal to herself.

'Really, Gerard, you are so violent in your opinions that I am sorry I spoke of Lady Rachel. Shall I find you equally prejudiced, and equally severe, if I change the subject to dear Lady Lena? Oh, don't say you think She is false, too!'

Here Mrs Roylake made her first mistake. She over-acted her part; and, when it was too late, she arrived, I suspect, at that conclusion herself.

'If you hav'n't seen that I sincerely admire Lady Lena,' I said, as smartly as I could, 'the sooner you disfigure yourself with a pair of spectacles, my dear lady, the better. She is very pretty, perfectly unaffected, and, if I may presume to judge, delightfully well-bred and well-dressed.'

My stepmother's face actually brightened with pleasure. Reflecting on it now, I am strongly disposed to think that she had not allowed her feelings to express themselves so unreservedly, since the time when she was a girl. After all, Mrs Roylake was paying her step-son a compliment in trying to entrap him into a splendid marriage. It was my duty to think kindly of my ambitious relative. I did my duty.

'You really like my sweet Lena?' she said. 'I am so glad. What were you talking about, with her? She made you exert all your powers of conversation, and she seemed to be deeply interested.'

More over-acting! Another mistake! And I could see through it! With no English subject which we could discuss in common, Lady Lena's ready tact alluded to my past life. Mrs Roylake had told her that I was educated at a German University. She had heard vaguely of students with long hair, who wore Hessian boots, and fought duels; and she appealed to my experience to tell her something more. I did my best to interest her, with very indifferent success, and was undeservedly rewarded by a patient attention, which presented the unselfish refinements of courtesy under their most perfect form.

But let me do my stepmother justice. She contrived to bend me to her will, before she left the smoking-room – I am sure I don't know how.

'You have entertained the charming daughters at dinner,' she reminded me; 'and the least you can do, after that, is to pay your respects to their noble father. In your position, my dear boy, you cannot neglect our English customs without producing the worst possible impression.'

In two words, I found myself pledged, under pretence of visiting my lord, to improve my acquaintance with Lady Lena on the next day.

'And pray be careful,' Mrs Roylake proceeded, still braving the atmosphere of the smoking-room, 'not to look surprised if you find Lord Uppercliff's house presenting rather a poor appearance just now.'

I was dying for another cigar, and I entirely misunderstood the words of warning which had just been addressed to me. I tried to bring our interview to a close by making a generous proposal.

'Does he want money?' I asked. 'I'll lend him some with the greatest pleasure.'

Mrs Roylake's horror expressed itself in a little thin wiry scream.

'Oh, Gerard, what people you must have lived among! What shocking ignorance of my lord's enormous fortune! He and his family have only just returned to their country seat, after a long absence – parliament you know, and foreign baths, and so on – and their English establishment is not yet complete. I don't know what mistake you may not make next. Do listen to what I want to say to you.'

Listening, I must acknowledge, with an absent mind, my attention was suddenly seized by Mrs Roylake – without the slightest conscious effort towards that end, on the part of the lady herself.

The first words that startled me, in her flow of speech, were these:

'And I must not forget to tell you of poor Lord Uppercliff's misfortune. He had a fall, some time since, and broke his leg. As I think, he was so unwise as to let a plausible young surgeon set the broken bone. Anyway, the end of it is that my lord slightly limps when he walks; and pray remember that he hates to see it noticed. Lady Rachel doesn't agree with me in attributing her father's lameness to his surgeon's want of experience. Between ourselves, the man seems to have interested her. Very handsome, very clever, very agreeable, and the manners of a gentleman. When his medical services came to an end, he was quite an acquisition at their parties in London – with one drawback: he mysteriously disappeared, and has never been heard of since. Ask Lady Lena about it. She will give you all the details, without her elder sister's bias in favour of the handsome young man. What a pretty compliment you are paying me! You really look as if I had interested you.'

Knowing what I knew, I was unquestionably interested.

Although the recent return of Lord Uppercliff and his daughter to their country home had, as yet, allowed no opportunity of a meeting, out of doors, between the deaf Lodger and the friends whom he had lost sight of – no doubt at the time of his serious illness – still, the inevitable discovery might happen on any day. What result would follow? And what would be the effect on Lady Rachel, when she met with the fascinating young surgeon, and discovered the terrible change in him?

CHAPTER X

WARNED!

We were alone in the glade, by the side of the spring. At that early hour there were no interruptions to dread; but Cristel was ill at ease. She seemed to be eager to get back to the cottage as soon as possible.

'Father tells me,' she began abruptly, 'he saw you at the boat-house. And it seemed to him, that you were behaving yourself like a friend to that terrible man.'

I reminded her of my having expressed the fear that we had been needlessly hard on him; and, I added that he had written a letter which confirmed me in that opinion. She looked, not only disappointed, but even alarmed.

'I had hoped,' she said sadly, 'that father was mistaken.'

'So little mistaken,' I assured her, 'that I am going to drink tea with the man who seems to frighten you. I hope he will ask you to meet me.'

She recoiled from the bare idea of an invitation.

'Will you hear what I want to tell you?' she said earnestly. 'You may alter your opinion if you know what I have been foolish enough to do, when you saw me go to the other side of the cottage.'

'Dear Cristel, I know what I owe to your kind interest in me on that occasion!' Before I could say a word of apology for having wronged her by my suspicions, she insisted on an explanation of what I had just said.

'Did he mention it in his letter?' she asked.

I owned that I had obtained my information in this way. And I declared that he had expressed his admiration of her, and his belief in her, in terms which made it a subject of regret to me not to be able to show what he had written.

Cristel forgot her fear of our being interrupted. Her dismay expressed itself in a cry that rang through the wood.

'You even believe in his letter?' she exclaimed. 'Mr Gerard! His writing in that way to You about Me is a proof that he lies; and I'll make you see it. If you were anybody else but yourself, I would leave you to your fate. Yes, your fate,' she passionately repeated. 'Oh, forgive me, sir! I'm behaving disrespectfully; I beg your pardon. No, no; let me go on. When I spoke to him in your best interests (as I did most truly believe) I never suspected what mischief I had done, till I looked in his face. Then, I saw how he hated you, and how vilely he was thinking in secret of me——'

Pure delusion! How could I allow it to go on? I interrupted her.

'My dear, you have quite mistaken him. As I have already said, he sincerely respects you – and he owns that he misjudged me when he and I first met.'

'What! Is *that* in his letter too? It's worse even than I feared. Again, and again, and again, I say it' – she stamped on the ground in the fervour of her conviction – 'he hates you with the hatred that never forgives and never forgets. You think him a good man. Do you suppose I would have begged and prayed of my father to send him away, without having reasons that justified me? Mr Gerard, you force me to tell you what my unlucky visit did put into his head. Yes, he does believe – believes firmly – that you have forgotten what is due to your rank; that I have been wicked enough to forget it too; and that you are going to take me away from him. Say what he may, and write what he may, he is deceiving you for his own wicked ends. If you go to drink tea with him, God only knows what cause you may have to regret it. Forgive me for being so violent, sir; I have done now. You have made me very wretched, but you are too good and kind to mean it. Good-bye.'

I took her hand, I pressed it tenderly; I was touched, deeply touched.

No! let me write honestly. Her eyes betrayed her, her voice betrayed her, while she said her parting words. What I saw, what I heard, was no longer within the limits of doubt. The sweet girl's interest in my welfare was not the merely friendly interest which she herself believed it to be. And I said just now that I was 'touched'. Cant! Lies! I loved her more dearly than I had ever loved her yet. There is the truth – stripped of poor prudery, and the mean fear of being called Vain!

What I might have said to her, if the opportunity had offered itself, may be easily imagined. Before I could open my lips, a man appeared on the path which led from the mill to the spring – the man whom Cristel had secretly suspected of a design to follow her.

I felt her hand trembling in my hand, and gave it a little encouraging squeeze. 'Let us judge him,' I suggested, 'by what he says and does, on finding us together.'

Without an attempt at concealment on his part, he advanced towards us briskly, smiling and waving his hand.

'What, Mr Roylake, you have already found out the virtues of your wonderful spring, and you are drinking the water before breakfast! I have often done it myself when I was not too lazy to get up. And this charming girl,' he went on, turning to Cristel, 'has she been trying the virtues of the spring by your advice? She won't listen to me, or I should have recommended it long since. See me set the example.'

He took a silver mug from his pocket, and descended the few steps that led to the spring. Allowing for the dreadful deaf monotony in his voice, no man could have been more innocently joyous and agreeable. While he was taking his morning draught, I appealed to Cristel's better sense.

'Is this the hypocrite, who is deceiving me for his own wicked ends?' I asked. 'Does he look like the jealous monster who is plotting my destruction, and who will succeed if I am fool enough to accept his invitation?'

Poor dear, she was as obstinate as ever! 'Think over what I have said to you – think, for your own sake,' was her only reply.

'And a little for *your* sake?' I ventured to add.

She ran away from me, taking the path which would lead her home again. The deaf man and I were left together. He looked after her until she was out of sight. Then he produced his book of blank leaves. But, instead of handing it to me as usual, he began to write in it himself.

'I have something to say to you,' he explained.

It was only possible, while the book was in his possession, to remind him that I could hear, and that he could speak, by using the language of signs. I touched my lips, and pointed to him; I touched my ear, and pointed to myself.

'Yes,' he said, understanding me with his customary quickness; 'but I want you to remember as well as to hear. When I have filled this leaf, I shall beg you to keep it about you, and to refer to it from time to time.'

He wrote on steadily, until he had filled both sides of the slip of paper.

'Quite a little letter,' he said. 'Pray read it.'

This is what I read:

'You must have seen for yourself that I was incapable of insulting you and Miss Cristel by an outbreak of jealousy, when I found you together just now. Only remember that we all have our weaknesses, and that it is my hard lot to be in a state of contest with the inherited evil which is the calamity of my life. With your encouragement, I may resist temptation in the future, and keep the better part of me in authority over my thoughts and actions. But, be on your guard, and advise Miss Cristel to be on her guard, against false appearances. As we all know, they lie like truth. Consider me. Pity me. I ask no more.'

Straightforward and manly and modest – I appeal to any unprejudiced mind whether I should not have committed a mean action, if I had placed an evil construction on this?

'Am I understood?' he asked.

I signed to him to give me his book, and relieved him of anxiety in these words:

'If I had failed to understand you, I should have felt ashamed of myself. May I show what you have written to Cristel?'

He smiled, more sweetly and pleasantly than I had seen him smile yet.

'If you wish it,' he answered. 'I leave it entirely to you. Thank you – and good morning.'

Having advanced a few steps on his way to the cottage, he paused, and reminded me of the tea-drinking: 'Don't forget to-morrow evening, at seven o'clock.'

CHAPTER XI

WARNED AGAIN!

The breakfast hour had not yet arrived when I got home. I went into the garden to refresh my eyes – a little weary of the solemn uniformity of colour in Fordwitch Wood – by looking at the flowers.

Reaching the terrace, in the first place, I heard below me a man's voice, speaking in tones of angry authority, and using language which expressed an intention of turning somebody out of the garden. I at once descended the steps which led to the flower-beds. The man in authority proved to be one of my gardeners; and the man threatened with instant expulsion was the oddly-dressed servant of the friend whom I had just left.

The poor fellow's ugly face presented a picture of shame and contrition, the moment I showed myself. He piteously entreated me to look over it, and to forgive him.

'Wait a little,' I said. 'Let me see if I have anything to forgive.' I turned to the gardener. 'What is your complaint of this man?'

'He's a trespasser on your grounds, sir. And, his impudence, to say the least of it, is such as I never met with before.'

'What harm has he done?'

'Harm, sir?'

'Yes – harm. Has he been picking the flowers?'

The gardener looked round him, longing to refer me to the necessary evidence, and failing to discover it anywhere. The wretched trespasser took heart of grace, and said a word in his own defence.

'Nobody ever knew me to misbehave myself in a gentleman's garden,' he said; 'I own, sir, to having taken a peep at the flowers, over the wall.'

'And they tempted you to look a little closer at them?'

'That's the truth, sir.'

'So you are fond of flowers?'

'Yes, sir. I once failed in business as a nurseryman – but I don't blame the flowers.'

The delightful simplicity of this was lost on the gardener. I heard the brute mutter to himself: 'Gammon!' For once I asserted my authority over my servant.

'Understand this,' I said to him: 'I don't confine the enjoyment of my garden to myself and my friends. Any well-behaved persons are welcome to come here and look at the flowers. Remember that. Now you may go.'

Having issued these instructions, I next addressed myself to my friend in the shabby shooting jacket; telling him to roam wherever he liked, and to stay as long as he pleased. Instead of thanking me and using his liberty, he hesitated, and looked thoroughly ill at ease.

'What's the matter now?' I asked.

'I'm afraid you don't know, sir, who it is you are so kind to. I've been something else in my time, besides a nurseryman.'

'What have you been?'

'A prize-fighter.'

If he expected me to exhibit indignation or contempt, he was disappointed. My ignorance treated him as civilly as ever.

'What is a prize-fighter?' I inquired.

The unfortunate pugilist looked at me in speechless bewilderment. I told him that I had been brought up among foreigners, and that I had never even seen an English newspaper for the last ten years. This explanation seemed to encourage the man of few words: it set him talking freely at last. He delivered a treatise on the art of prize-fighting, and he did something else which I found more amusing – he told me his name. To my small sense of humour his name, so to speak, completed this delightfully odd man: it was Gloody. As to the list of his misfortunes, the endless length of it became so unendurably droll, that we both indulged in unfeeling fits of laughter over the sorrows of Gloody. The first lucky accident of the poor fellow's life had been, literally, the discovery of him by his present master.

This event interested me. I said I should like to hear how it had happened.

Gloody modestly described himself as 'one of the starving lot, sir, that looks out for small errands. I got my first dinner for three days, by carrying a gentleman's portmanteau for him. And he, if you please, was afterwards my master. He lived alone. Bless you, he was as deaf then as he is now. He says to me, 'If you bawl in my ears, I'll knock you down.' I thought to myself, you wouldn't say that, master, if you knew how I was employed twenty years ago. He took me into his service, sir, because I was ugly. 'I'm so handsome myself,' he says, 'I want a contrast of something ugly about me.' You may have noticed that he's a bitter one – and bitterly enough he sometimes behaved to me. But there's a good side to him. He gives me his old clothes, and sometimes he speaks almost as kindly to me as you do. But for him, I believe I should have perished of starvation——'

He suddenly checked himself. Whether he was afraid of wearying me, or whether some painful recollection had occurred to him, it was of course impossible to say.

The ugly face, to which he owed his first poor little morsel of prosperity became overclouded by care and doubt. Bursting into expressions of gratitude which I had certainly not deserved – expressions, so evidently sincere, that they bore witness to constant ill-usage suffered in the course of his hard life – he left me with a headlong haste of movement, driven away as I fancied by an unquiet mind.

I watched him retreating along the path, and saw him stop abruptly, still with his back to me. His deep strong voice travelled farther than he supposed. I heard him say to himself: 'What an infernal rascal I am!' He waited a little, and turned my way again. Slowly and reluctantly, he came back to me. As he approached I saw the man, who had lived by the public exhibition of his courage, looking at me with fear plainly visible in the change of his colour, and the expression of his face.

'Anything wrong?' I inquired.

'Nothing wrong, sir. Might I be so bold as to ask——'

We waited a little; I gave him time to collect his thoughts. Perhaps the silence confused him. Anyhow, I was obliged to help him to get on.

'What do you wish to ask of me?' I said.

'I wished to speak, sir——!'

He stopped again.

'About what?' I asked.

'About to-morrow evening.'

'Well?'

He burst out with it, at last. 'Are you coming to drink tea with my master?'

'Of course, I am coming! Mr Gloody, do you know that you rather surprise me?'

'I hope no offence, sir.'

'Nonsense! It seems odd, my good fellow, that your master shouldn't have told you I was coming to drink tea with him. Isn't it your business to get the things ready?'

He shifted from one foot to another, and looked as if he wished himself out of my way. At a later time of my life, I have observed that these are signs by which an honest man is apt to confess that he has told, or is going to tell, a lie. As it was, I only noticed that he answered confusedly.

'I can't quite say, Mr Roylake, that my master didn't mention the thing to me.'

'But you failed to understand him – is that it?'

'Well, sir, if I want to ask him anything I have to write it. I'm slow at writing, and bad at writing, and he isn't always patient. However, as you reminded me just now, I have got to get the things ready. To cut it short, perhaps I might say that I didn't quite expect the tea-party would come off.'

'Why shouldn't it come off?'

'Well, sir, you might have some other engagement.'

Was this a hint? or only an excuse? In either case it was high time, if he still refused to speak out, that I should set him the example.

'You have given me some curious information,' I said, 'on the subject of fighting with the fists; and you have made me understand the difference between "fair hitting" and "foul hitting". Are you hitting fair now? Very likely I am mistaken – but you seem to me to be trying to prevent my accepting your master's invitation.'

He pulled off his hat in a hurry.

'I beg your pardon, sir; I won't detain you any longer. If you will allow me, I'll take my leave.'

'Don't go, Mr Gloody, without telling me whether I am right or wrong. Is there really some objection to my coming to tea to-morrow?'

'Quite a mistake, sir,' he said, still in a hurry. 'I've led you wrong without meaning it – being an ignorant man, and not knowing how to express myself. Don't think me ungrateful, Mr Roylake! After your kindness to me, I'd go through fire and water for you – I would!'

His sunken eyes moistened, his big voice faltered. I let him leave me, in mercy to the strong feeling which I had innocently roused. But I shook hands with him first. Yielding to one of my headlong impulses? Yes. And doing a very indiscreet thing? Wait a little – and we shall see.

CHAPTER XII

WARNED FOR THE LAST TIME!

My loyalty towards the afflicted man, whose friendly advances I had seen good reason to return, was in no sense shaken. His undeserved misfortunes, his manly appeal to me at the spring, his hopeless attachment to the beautiful girl whose aversion towards him I had unhappily encouraged, all pleaded with me in his favour. I had accepted his invitation; and I had no other engagement to claim me: it would have been an act of meanness amounting to a confession of fear, if I had sent an excuse. Still, while Cristel's entreaties and Cristel's influence had failed to shake me, Gloody's strange language and Gloody's incomprehensible conduct had troubled my mind. I felt vaguely uneasy; irritated by my own depression of spirits. If I had been a philosopher, I should have recognized the symptoms of a very common attack of a very widely-spread moral malady. The meanest of all human infirmities is also the most universal; and the name of it is Self-esteem.

It is perhaps only right to add that my patience had been tried by the progress of domestic events, which affected Lady Lena and myself – viewed as victims.

Calling, with my stepmother, at Lord Uppercliff's house later in the day, I perceived that Lady Rachel and Mrs Roylake found (or made) an opportunity of talking together confidentially in a corner; and, once or twice, I caught them looking at Lady Lena and at me. Even Lord Uppercliff (perhaps not yet taken into their confidence) noticed the proceedings of the two ladies, and seemed to be at a loss to understand them.

When Mrs Roylake and I were together again, on our way home, I was prepared to hear the praise of Lady Lena, followed by a delicate examination into the state of my heart.

Neither of these anticipations was realized. Once more, my clever stepmother had puzzled me.

Mrs Roylake talked as fluently as ever; exhausting one common-place subject after another, without the slightest allusion to my lord's daughter, to my matrimonial prospects, or to my visits at the mill. I was secretly annoyed, feeling that my stepmother's singular indifference to domestic interests of paramount importance, at other times, must have some object in view, entirely beyond the reach of my penetration. If I had dared to commit such an act of rudeness, I should have jumped out of the carriage, and have told Mrs Roylake that I meant to walk home.

The day was Sunday. I loitered about the garden, listening to the distant church-bell ringing for the afternoon service. Without any cause that I knew of to account for it, I was so restless that nothing I could do attracted me or quieted me.

Returning to the house, I tried to occupy myself with my collection of insects, sadly neglected of late. Useless! My own moths failed to interest me.

I went back to the garden. Passing the open window of one of the lower rooms which looked out on the terrace, I saw Mrs Roylake reading a book in sad-coloured binding. She was yawning over it fearfully, when she discovered that I was looking at her. Equal to any emergency, this remarkable woman instantly handed to me a second and similar volume. 'The most precious sermons, Gerard, that have been written in our time.' I looked at the book; I opened the book; I recovered my presence of mind, and handed it back. If a female humbug was on one side of the window, a male humbug was on the other. 'Please keep it for me till the evening,' I said; 'I am going for a walk.'

Which way did I turn my steps?

Men will wonder what possessed me – women will think it a proceeding that did me credit – I took the familiar road which led to the gloomy wood and the guilty river. The longing in me to see Cristel again, was more than I could resist. Not because I was in love with her; only because I had left her in distress.

Beyond the spring, and within a short distance of the river, I saw a lady advancing towards me on the path which led from the mill.

Brisk, smiling, tripping along like a young girl, behold the mock-republican, known in our neighbourhood as Lady Rachel! She held out both hands to me. But for her petticoats, I should have thought I had met with a jolly young man.

'I have been wandering in your glorious wood, Mr Roylake. Anything to escape the respectable classes on Sunday, patronizing piety on the way to afternoon church. I must positively make a sketch of the cottage by the mill – I mean, of course, the picturesque side it. That fine girl of Toller's was standing at the door. She is really handsomer than ever. Are you going to see her, you wicked man? Which do you admire – that gipsy complexion, or Lena's lovely skin? Both, I have no doubt, at your age. Good-bye.'

When we had left each other, I thought of the absent Captain in the Navy who was Lady Rachel's husband. He was a perfect stranger – but I put myself in his place, and felt that I too should have gone to sea.

Old Toller was alone in his kitchen, evidently annoyed and angry.

'We are all at sixes and sevens, Mr Gerard. I've had another row with that deaf-devil – my new name for him, and I think it's rather clever. He swears, sir, that he won't go at the end of his week's notice. Says, if I think I'm likely to get rid of him before he has married Cristy, I'm mistaken. Threatens, if any man attempts to take her away, he'll shoot her, and shoot the man, and shoot himself. Aha! old as I am, if he believes he's going to have it all his own way, he's mistaken. I'll be even with him. You mark my words: I'll be even with him.'

That old Toller – the most exasperating of men, judged by a quick temper – had irritated my friend into speaking rashly was plain enough. Nevertheless, I felt some anxiety (jealous anxiety, I am afraid) about Cristel. After looking round the kitchen again, I asked where she was.

'Sitting forlorn in her bedroom, crying,' her father told me. 'I went out for a walk by the river, and I sat down, and (being Sunday) I fell asleep. When I woke, and got home again just now, that was how I found her. I don't like to hear my girl crying; she's as good as gold and better. No, sir; our deaf-devil is not to blame for this. He has given Cristy no reason to complain of him. She says so herself – and she never told a lie yet.'

'But, Mr Toller,' I objected, 'something must have happened to distress her. Has she not told you what it is?'

'Not she! Obstinate about it. Leaves me to guess. It's
clear to my mind, Mr Gerard, that somebody has got at her
in my absence, and said something to upset her. You will
ask me who the person is. I can't say I have found that out
yet.'

'But you mean to try?'

'Yes; I mean to try.'

He answered me with little of the energy which generally
distinguished him. Perhaps he was fatigued, or perhaps he had
something else to think of. I offered a suggestion.

'When we are in want of help,' I said, 'we sometimes find it,
nearer than we had ventured to expect – at our own doors.'

The ancient miller rose at that hint like a fish at a fly.

'Gloody!' he cried.

'Find him at once, Mr Toller.'

He hobbled to the door – and looked round at me. 'I've got
burdens on my mind,' he explained, 'or I should have thought
of it too.' Having done justice to his own abilities, he bustled
out. In less than a minute, he was back again in a state of
breathless triumph. 'Gloody has seen the person,' he
announced; 'and (what do you think, sir?) it's a woman!'

I beckoned to Gloody, waiting modestly at the door, to
come in, and tell me what he had discovered.

'I saw her outside, sir – rapping at the door here, with her
parasol.' That was the servant's report.

Her parasol? Not being acquainted with the development of
dress among female servants in England, I asked if she was a
lady. There seemed to be no doubt of it in the man's mind.
She was also, as Gloody supposed, a person whom he had
never seen before.

'How is it you are not sure of that?' I said.

'Well, sir, she was waiting to be let in; and I was behind her,
coming out of the wood.'

'Who let her in?'

'Miss Cristel.' His face brightened with an expression of
interest when he mentioned the miller's daughter. He went
on with his story without wanting questions to help him.
'Miss Cristel looked like a person surprised at seeing a

stranger – what *I* should call a free and easy stranger. She walked in, sir, as if the place belonged to her.'

I am not suspicious by nature, as I hope and believe. But I began to be reminded of Lady Rachel already.

'Did you notice the lady's dress?' I asked.

A woman who had seen her would have been able to describe every morsel of her dress from head to foot. The man had only observed her hat; and all he could say was that he thought it 'a smartish one'.

'Any particular colour?' I went on.

'Not that I know of. Dark green, I think.'

'Any ornament in it?'

'Yes! A purple feather.'

The hat I had seen on the head of that hateful woman was now sufficiently described – for a man. Sly old Toller, leaving Gloody unnoticed, and keeping his eye on me, saw the signs of conviction in my face, and said with his customary audacity: 'Who is she?'

I followed, at my humble distance, the example of Sir Walter Scott, when inquisitive people asked him if he was the author of the Waverley Novels. In plain English, I denied all knowledge of the stranger wearing the green hat. But, I was naturally desirous of discovering next what Lady Rachel had said; and I asked to speak with Cristel. Her far-seeing father might or might not have perceived a chance of listening to our conversation. He led me to the door of his daughter's room; and stood close by, when I knocked softly, and begged that she would come out.

The tone of the poor girl's voice – answering, 'Forgive me, sir; I can't do it' – convicted the she-socialist (as I thought) of merciless conduct of some sort. Assuming this conclusion to be the right one, I determined, then and there, that Lady Rachel should not pass the doors of Trimley Deen again. If her bosom-friend resented that wise act of severity by leaving the house, I should submit with resignation, and should remember the circumstance with pleasure.

'I am afraid you are ill, Cristel?' was all I could find to say, under the double disadvantage of speaking through a door, and having a father listening at my side.

'Oh no, Mr Gerard, not ill. A little low in my mind, that's all. I don't mean to be rude, sir – pray be kinder to me than ever! pray let me be!'

I said I would return on the next day; and left the room with a sore heart.

Old Toller highly approved of my conduct. He rubbed his fleshless hands, and whispered: 'You'll get it out of Cristy to-morrow, and I'll help you.'

I found Gloody waiting for me outside the cottage. He was anxious about Miss Cristel; his only excuse, he told me, being the fear that she might be ill. Having set him at ease, in that particular, I said: 'You seem to be interested in Miss Cristel.'

His answer raised him a step higher in my estimation.

'How can I help it, sir?'

An odd man, with a personal appearance that might excite a prejudice against him, in some minds. I failed to see it myself in that light. It struck me, as I walked home, that Cristel might have made many a worse friend than the retired prize-fighter.

A change in my manner was of course remarked by Mrs Roylake's ready observation. I told her that I had been annoyed, and offered no other explanation. Wonderful to relate, she showed no curiosity and no surprise. More wonderful still, at every fair opportunity that offered, she kept out of my way.

My next day's engagement being for seven o'clock in the evening, I put Mrs Roylake's self-control to a new test. With prefatory excuses, I informed her that I should not be able to dine at home as usual. Impossible as it was that she could have been prepared to hear this, her presence of mind was equal to the occasion. I left the house, followed by my stepmother's best wishes for a pleasant evening.

Hoping to speak with Cristel alone, I had arranged to reach the cottage before seven o'clock.

On the river-margin of the wood, I was confronted by a wild gleam of beauty in the familiar view, for which previous experience had not prepared me. Am I wrong in believing that all scenery, no matter how magnificent or how homely it may be, derives a splendour not its own from favouring conditions of light and shade? Our gloomy trees and our repellent river presented an aspect superbly transfigured, under the shadows of the towering clouds, the fantastic wreaths of the mist, and the lurid reddening of the sun as it stooped to its setting.

Lovely interfusions of sobered colour rested, faded, returned again, on the upper leaves of the foliage as they lightly moved. The mist, rolling capriciously over the waters, revealed the grandly deliberate course of the flowing current, while it dimmed the turbid earthy yellow that discoloured and degraded the stream under the full glare of day. While my eyes followed the successive transformations of the view, as the hour advanced, tender and solemn influences breathed their balm over my mind. Days, happy days that were past, revived. Again, I walked hand in hand with my mother, among the scenes that were round me, and learnt from her to be grateful for the beauty of the earth, with a heart that felt it. We were tracing our way along our favourite woodland path; and we found a companion of tender years, hiding from us. She showed herself, blushing, hesitating, offering a nosegay of wild flowers. My mother whispered to me – I thanked the little mill-girl, and gave her a kiss. Did I feel the child's breath, in my day-dream, still fluttering on my cheek? Was I conscious of her touch? I started, trembled, returned reluctantly to my present self. A visible hand touched my arm. As I turned suddenly, a living breath played on my face. The child had faded into a vanishing shade: the perfected woman who had grown from her had stolen on me unawares, and was asking me to pardon her. 'Mr Gerard, you were lost in your thoughts; I spoke, and you never heard me.'

I looked at her in silence.

Was this the dear Cristel so well known to me? Or was it a mockery of her that had taken her place?

'I hope I have not offended you?' she said.

'You have surprised me,' I answered. 'Something must have happened, since I saw you last. What is it?'

'Nothing.'

I advanced a step, and drew her closer to me. A dark flush discoloured her face. An overpowering brilliancy flashed from her eyes; there was an hysterical defiance in her manner. 'Are you excited? are you angry? are you trying to startle me by acting a part?' I urged those questions on her, one after another; and I was loudly and confidently answered.

'I dare say I am excited, Mr Gerard, by the honour that has been done me. You are going to keep your engagement, of

course? Well, your friend, your favourite friend, has invited
me to meet you. No! that's not quite true. I invited myself –
the deaf gentleman submitted.'

'Why did you invite yourself?'

'Because a tea-party is not complete without a woman.'

Her manner was as strangely altered as her looks. That she
was beside herself for the moment, I clearly saw. That she had
answered me unreservedly, it was impossible to believe. I
began to feel angry, when I ought to have made allowances for
her.

'Is this Lady Rachel's doing?' I said.

'What do you know of Lady Rachel, sir?'

'I know that she has visited you, and spoken to you.'

'Do you know what she has said?'

'I can guess.'

'Mr Gerard, don't abuse that good and kind lady. She
deserves your gratitude as well as mine.'

Her manner had become quieter; her face was more composed; her expression almost recovered its natural charm
while she spoke of Lady Rachel. I was stupefied.

'Try, sir, to forget it and forgive it,' she resumed gently, 'if I
have misbehaved myself. I don't rightly know what I am
saying or doing.'

I pointed to the new side of the cottage, behind us.

'Is the cause there?' I asked.

'No! no indeed! I have not seen him; I have not heard from
him. His servant often brings me messages. Not one message
to-day.'

'Have you seen Gloody to-day?'

'Oh, yes! There's one thing, if I may make so bold, I should
like to know. Mr Gloody is as good to me as good can be; we
see each other continually, living in the same place. But you
are different; and he tells me himself he has only seen you
twice. What have you done, Mr Gerard, to make him like you
so well, in that short time?'

I told her that he had been found in my garden, looking at
the flowers. 'As he had done no harm,' I said, 'I wouldn't
allow the servant to turn him out; and I walked round the
flower-beds with him. Little enough to deserve such gratitude
as the poor fellow expressed – and felt, I don't doubt it.'

I had intended to say no more than this. But the remembrance of Gloody's mysterious prevarication, and of the uneasiness which I had undoubtedly felt when I thought of it afterwards, led me (I cannot pretend to say how) into associating Cristel's agitation with something which this man might have said to her. I was on the point of putting the question, when she held up her hand, and said, 'Hush!'

The wind was blowing towards us from the river-side village, to which I have already alluded. I am not sure whether I have mentioned that the name of the place was Kylam. It was situated behind a promontory of the river-bank, clothed thickly with trees, and was not visible from the mill. In the present direction of the wind, we could hear the striking of the church clock. Cristel counted the strokes.

'Seven,' she said. 'Are you determined to keep your engagement?'

She had repeated – in an unsteady voice, and with a sudden change in her colour to paleness – the strange question put to me by Gloody. In his case I had failed to trace the motive. I tried to discover it now.

'Tell me why I ought to break my engagement,' I said.

'Remember what I told you at the spring,' she answered. 'You are deceived by a false friend who lies to you and hates you.'

The man she was speaking of turned the corner of the new cottage. He waved his hand gaily, and approached us along the road.

'Go!' she said. 'Your guardian angel has forgotten you. It's too late now.'

Instead of letting me precede her, as I had anticipated, she ran on before me – made a sign to the deaf man, as she passed him, not to stop her – and disappeared through the open door of her father's side of the cottage.

I was left to decide for myself. What should I have done, if I had been twenty years older?

Say that my moral courage would have risen superior to the poorest of all fears, the fear of appearing to be afraid, and that I should have made my excuses to my host of the evening – how would my moral courage have answered him, if he had asked for an explanation? Useless to speculate on it! Had I possessed the wisdom of middle life, his book of leaves would not have told him, in my own handwriting, that I believed in his better nature, and accepted his friendly letter in the spirit in which he had written it.

Explain it who can – I knew that I was going to drink tea with him, and yet I was unwilling to advance a few steps, and meet him on the road!

'I find a new bond of union between us,' he said, as he joined me. 'We both feel *that*.' He pointed to the grandly darkening view. 'The two men who could have painted the mystery of those growing shadows and fading lights, lie in the graves of Rembrandt and Turner. Shall we go to tea?'

On our way to his room we stopped at the miller's door.

'Will *you* inquire,' he said, 'if Miss Cristel is ready?'

I went in. Old Toller was in the kitchen, smoking his pipe without appearing to enjoy it.

'What's come to my girl?' he asked, the moment he saw me. 'Yesterday she was in her room, crying. To-day she's in her room, praying.'

The warnings which I had neglected rose in judgment against me. I was silent; I was awed. Before I recovered myself, Cristel entered the kitchen. Her father whispered, 'Look at her!'

Of the excitement which had disturbed – I had almost said, profaned – her beautiful face, not a vestige remained. Pale, composed, resolute, she said, 'I am ready,' and led the way out.

The man whom she hated offered his arm. She took it!

CHAPTER XIII

THE CLARET JUG

I perceived but one change in The Lodger's miserable room, since I had seen it last.

A second table was set against one of the walls. Our boiling water for the tea was kept there, in a silver kettle heated by a spirit-lamp. I next observed a delicate little china vase which held the tea, and a finely-designed glass claret jug, with a silver cover. Other men, possessing that beautiful object, would have thought it worthy of the purest Bordeaux wine which the arts of modern adulteration permit us to drink. This man had filled the claret jug with water.

'All my valuable property, ostentatiously exposed to view,' he said, in his bitterly facetious manner. 'My landlord's property matches it on the big table.'

The big table presented a coarse earthenware teapot; cups and saucers with pieces chipped out of them; a cracked milk jug; a tumbler which served as a sugar basin; and an old vegetable dish, honoured by holding delicate French sweet-meats for the first time since it had left the shop.

My deaf friend, in boisterously good spirits, pointed backwards and forwards between the precious and the worthless objects on the two tables, as if he saw a prospect that delighted him.

'I don't believe the man lives,' he said, 'who enjoys Contrast as I do. – What do you want now?'

This question was addressed to Gloody, who had just entered the room. He touched the earthenware teapot. His master answered: 'Let it alone.'

'I make the tea at other times,' the man persisted, looking at me.

'What does he say? Write it down for me, Mr Roylake. I beg you will write it down.'

There was anger in his eyes as he made that request. I took his book, and wrote the words – harmless words, surely? He read them, and turned savagely to his unfortunate servant.

'In the days when you were a ruffian in the prize-ring, did the other men's fists beat all the brains out of your head? Do you think you can make tea that is fit for Mr Roylake to drink?'

He pointed to an open door, communicating with another bedroom. Gloody's eyes rested steadily on Cristel: she failed to notice him, being occupied at the moment in replacing the pin of a brooch which had slipped out of her dress. The man withdrew into the second bedroom, and softly closed the door.

Our host recovered his good humour. He took a wooden stool, and seated himself by Cristel.

'Borrowed furniture,' he said, 'as well as borrowed tea-things. What a debt of obligation I owe to your excellent father. How quiet you are, dear girl. Do you regret having followed the impulse which made you kindly offer to drink tea with us?' He suddenly turned to me. 'Another proof, Mr Roylake, of the sisterly interest that she feels in you; she can't hear of your coming to my room, without wanting to be with you. Ah, you possess the mysterious attractions which fasci-nate the sex. One of these days, *some* woman will love you as never man was loved yet.' He addressed himself again to Cristel. 'Still out of spirits? I dare say you are tired of waiting for your tea. No? You have had tea already? It's Gloody's fault; he ought to have told me that seven o'clock was too late for you. The poor devil deserved that you should take no notice of him when he looked at you just now. Are you one of the few women who dislike an ugly man? Women in general, I can tell you, prefer ugly men. A handsome man matches them on their own ground, and they don't like that. "We are so fond of our ugly husbands; they set us off to such advantage." Oh, I don't report what they say; I speak the language in which they think. – Mr Roylake, does it strike you that The Cur is a sad cynic? By-the-by, do you call me "The Cur" (as I suggested) when you speak of me to other people – to Miss Cristel, for instance? My charming young friends, you both look shocked; you both shake your heads. Perhaps I am in one of my tolerant humours to-day; I see nothing disgraceful in being a Cur. He is a dog who represents different breeds. Very well, the English are a people who represent different breeds: Saxons, Normans, Danes. The consequence, in one case, is a great nation. The consequence, in the other case, is the cleverest member of the whole dog family – as you may find out for yourself if you will only teach him. Ha – how I am running on. My guests try to slip in a word or two, and can't find their opportunity. Enjoyment, Miss Cristel. Excitement, Mr Roylake. For more than a year past, I have not luxuriated in the pleasures of society. I feel the social glow; I love the human family; I never, never, never was such a good man as I am now. Let vile slang express my emotions: isn't it jolly?'

Cristel and I stopped him, at the same moment. We instinctively lifted our hands to our ears.

In his delirium of high spirits, he had burst through the invariable monotony of his articulation. Without the slightest gradation of sound, his voice broke suddenly into a screech, prolonged in its own discord until it became perfectly unendurable to hear. The effect that he had produced upon us was not lost on him. His head sank on his breast; horrid shudderings shook him without mercy; he said to himself, not to us:

'I had forgotten I was deaf.'

There was a whole world of misery in those simple words. Cristel kept her place, unmoved. I rose, and put my hand kindly on his shoulder. It was the best way I could devise of assuring him of my sympathy.

He looked up at me, in silence.

His book of leaves was on the table; he did once more, what he had already done at the spring. Instead of using the book as usual, he wrote in it himself, and then handed it to me.

'Let me spare your nerves a repetition of my deaf discord. Sight, smell, touch, taste – I would give them all to be able to hear. In reminding me of that vain aspiration, my infirmity revenges itself: my deafness is not accustomed to be forgotten. Well! I can be silently useful; I can make the tea.'

He rose, and, taking the teapot with him, went to the table that had been placed against the wall. In that position, his back was turned towards us.

At the same time, I felt his book gently taken out of my hand. Cristel had been reading, while I read, over my shoulder. She wrote on the next blank leaf: 'Shall I make the tea?'

'Now,' she said to me, 'notice what happens.'

Following him, she touched his arm, and presented her request. He shook his head in token of refusal. She came back to her place by me.

'You expected that?' I said.

'Yes.'

'Why did you ask me to notice his refusal.'

'Because I may want to remind you that he wouldn't let me make the tea.'

'Mysteries, my dear?'

'Yes: mysteries.'

'Not to be mentioned more particularly?'

'I will mention one of them more particularly. After the tea has been made, you may possibly feel me touch your knee under the table.'

I was fool enough to smile at this, and wise enough afterwards to see in her face that I had made a mistake.

'What is your touch intended to mean?' I asked.

'It means, "Wait," she said.

My sense of humour was, by this time, completely held in check. That some surprise was in store for me, and that Cristel was resolved not to take me into her confidence, were conclusions at which I naturally arrived. I felt, and surely not without good cause, a little annoyed. The Lodger came back to us with the tea made. As he put the teapot on the table, he apologized to Cristel.

'Don't think me rude, in refusing your kind offer. If there is one thing I know I can do better than anybody else, that thing is making tea. Do you take sugar and milk, Mr Roylake?'

I made the affirmative sign. He poured out the tea. When he had filled two cups, the supply was exhausted. Cristel and I noticed this. He saw it, and at once gratified our curiosity.

'It is a rule,' he said, 'with masters in the art of making tea, that one infusion ought never to be used twice. If we want any more, we will make more; and if you feel inclined to join us, Miss Cristel, we will fill the third cup.'

What was there in this (I wondered) to make her turn pale? And why, after what he had just said, did I see her eyes willingly rest on him, for the first time in my experience? Entirely at a loss to understand her, I resignedly stirred my tea. On the point of tasting it next, I felt her hand on my knee, under the table.

Bewildered as I was, I obeyed my instructions, and went on stirring my tea. Our host smiled.

'Your sugar takes a long time to melt,' he said – and drank his tea. As he emptied the cup, the touch was taken off me. I followed his example.

In spite of his boasting, the tea was the worst I ever tasted. I should have thrown it out of the window, if they had offered us such nasty stuff at Trimley Deen. When I set down my cup, he asked facetiously if I wished him to brew any more. My negative answer was a masterpiece of strong expression, in the language of signs.

Instead of sending for Gloody to clear the table, he moved away the objects near him, so as to leave an empty space at his disposal.

'I ought perhaps to have hesitated, before I asked you to spend the evening with me,' he said, speaking with a gentleness and amiability of manner, strongly in contrast with his behaviour up to this time. 'It is my misfortune, as you both well know, to be a check on conversation. I dare say you have asked yourselves: How is he going to amuse us, after tea? If you will allow me, I propose to amuse you by exhibiting the dexterity of my fingers and thumbs. Before I was deaf, I should have preferred the piano for this purpose. As it is, an inferior accomplishment must serve my turn.'

He opened a cupboard in the wall, close by the second table, and returned with a pack of cards.

Cristel imitated the action of dealing cards for a game. 'No,' he said, 'that is not the amusement which I have in view. Allow me to present myself in a new character. I am no longer The Lodger, and no longer The Cur. My new name is more honourable still – I am The Conjurer.'

He shuffled the pack by pouring it backwards and forwards from one hand to the other, in a cascade of cards. The wonderful ease with which he did it prepared me for something worth seeing. Cristel's admiration of his dexterity expressed itself by a prolonged clapping of hands, and a strange uneasy laugh. As his excitement subsided, her agitation broke out. I saw the flush again on her face, and the fiery brightness in her eyes. Once, when his attention was engaged, she stole a look at the door by which Gloody had left the room. Did this indicate another of the mysteries which, by her own confession, she had in preparation for me? My late experience had not inclined me favourably towards mysteries. I devoted my whole attention to The Conjurer.

Whether he chose the easiest examples of skill in sleight of hand is more than I know. I can only say that I never was more completely mystified by any professor of legerdemain on the public platform. After the performance of each trick, he asked leave to 'time himself' by looking at his watch; being anxious to discover if he had lost his customary quickness of execution through recent neglect of the necessary practice.

Of Cristel's conduct, while he was amusing us, I can only say that it justified Mrs Roylake's spiteful description of her as a bold girl. The more cleverly the tricks were performed, the more they seemed to annoy and provoke her.

'I hate being puzzled!' she said, addressing herself of course to me. 'Yes, yes; his fingers are quicker than my eyes – I have heard that explanation before. When he has done one of his tricks, I want to know how he does it. Conjurers are people who ask riddles, and, when one can't guess them, refuse to say what the answer is. It's as bad as calling me a fool, to suppose that I like being deceived. Ah,' she cried, with a shocking insolence of look and manner, 'if our friend could only hear what I am saying!'

He had paused while she was speaking, observing her attentively. 'Your face doesn't encourage me,' he said, with a patience and courtesy of manner which it was impossible not to admire. 'I am coming gradually to my greatest triumph; and I think I can surprise and please you.'

He timed his last trick, and returned to the table placed against the wall.

'Excuse me for a moment,' he resumed; 'I am suffering as usual, after drinking tea. I so delight in it that the temptation to-night was more than I could resist. Tea disagrees with my weak stomach. It always produces thirst.'

'What nonsense he talks!' Cristel exclaimed. 'All mere fancy! He reminds me of the old song called 'The Nervous Man.' Do you know it, Mr Roylake?'

In spite of my efforts to prevent her, she burst out with the first verse of a stupid comic song. Spared by his deafness from this infliction of vulgarity, our host filled a tumbler from the water in the claret jug, and drank it.

As he set the tumbler down, we were startled by an accident in the next room. The floor was suddenly shaken by the sound of a heavy fall. The fall was followed by a groan which instantly brought me to my feet.

Although his infirmity made him unconscious of the groan, my friend felt the vibration of the floor, and saw me start up from my chair. He looked even more alarmed than I was, judging by the ghastly change that I saw in his colour; and he reached the door of the second room as soon as I did. It is needless to say that I allowed him to enter first.

On the point of following him, I felt myself roughly pulled back. When I turned round, and saw Cristel, I did really and truly believe that she was mad. The furious impatience in her eyes, the frenzied strength of her grasp on my arm, would have led most other men to form the same conclusion.

'Come!' she cried. 'No! not a word. There isn't a moment to lose.'

She dragged me across the room to the table on which the claret jug stood. She filled the tumbler from it, as *he* had filled the tumbler. The material of which the jug had been made was so solid (crystal, not glass as I had supposed) that the filling of the two tumblers emptied it. Cristel held the water out to me, gasping for breath, trembling as if she saw some frightful reptile before her instead of myself.

'Drink it,' she said, 'if you value your life!'

I should of course have found it perfectly easy to obey her, strange as her language was, if I had been in full possession of myself. Between distress and alarm, my mind (I suppose) had lost its balance. With or without a cause, I hesitated.

She crossed the room, and threw open the window which looked out on the river.

'You shan't die alone,' she said. 'If you don't drink it, I'll throw myself out!'

I drank from the tumbler to the last drop.

It was not water.

It had a taste which I can compare to no drink, and to no medicine, known to me. I thought of the other strange taste peculiar to the tea. At last, the tremendous truth forced itself on my mind. The man in whom my boyish generosity had so faithfully believed had attempted my life.

Cristel took the tumbler from me. My poor angel clasped her free arm round my neck, and pressed her lips, in an ecstasy of joy, on my cheek. The next instant, she seized the claret jug, and dashed it into pieces on the floor. 'Get the jug from his washhand-stand,' she said. When I gave it to her, she poured some of the water upon the broken fragments of crystal scattered on the floor. I had put the jug back in its place, and was returning to Cristel, when the poisoner showed himself, entering from the servant's room.

'Don't be alarmed,' he said. 'Gloody's name ought to be Glutton. An attack of giddiness, thoroughly well deserved. I have relieved him. You remember, Mr Roylake, that I was once a surgeon——'

The broken claret jug caught his eye.

We have all read of men who were petrified by terror. Of the few persons who have really witnessed that spectacle, I am one. The utter stillness of him was really terrible to see. Cristel wrote in his book an excuse, no doubt prepared beforehand: 'That fall in the next room frightened me, and I felt faint. I went to get some water from the jug you drank out of, and it slipped from my hand.'

She placed those words under his eyes – she might just as well have shown them to the dog. A dead man, erect on his feet – so he looked to our eyes. So he still looked, when I took Cristel's arm, and led her out of that dreadful presence.

'Take me into the air!' she whispered.

A burst of tears relieved her, after the unutterable suspense that she had so bravely endured. When she was in some degree composed again, we walked gently up and down for a minute or two in the cool night air. 'Don't speak to me,' she said, as we stopped before her father's door. 'I am not fit for it yet; I know what you feel.' I pressed her to my heart, and let the embrace speak for me. She yielded to it, faintly sighing. 'To-morrow?' I whispered. She bent her head, and left me.

Walking home through the wood, I became aware, little by little, that my thoughts were not under the customary control. Over and over again, I tried to review the events of that terrible evening, and failed. Fragments of other memories presented themselves – and then deserted me. Nonsense, absolute nonsense, found its way into my mind next, and rose in idiotic words to my lips. I grew too lazy even to talk to myself. I strayed from the path. The mossy earth began to rise and sink under my feet, like the waters in a ground-swell at sea. I stood still, in a state of idiot-wonder. The ground suddenly rose right up to my face. I remember no more.

My first conscious exercise of my senses, when I revived, came to me by way of my ears. Leaden weights seemed to close my eyes, to fetter my movements, to silence my tongue, to paralyse my touch. But I heard a wailing voice, speaking close to me, so close that it might have been my own voice: I distinguished the words; I knew the tones.

'Oh, my master, my lord, who am I that I should live – and you die! and you die!'

Was it her warm young breath that quickened me with its vigorous life? I only know that the revival of my sense of touch did certainly spring from the contact of her lips, pressed to mine in the reckless abandonment of grief without hope. Her cry of joy, when my first sigh told her that I was still a living creature, ran through me like an electric shock. I opened my eyes; I held out my hand; I tried to help her when she raised my head, and set me against the tree under which I had been stretched helpless. With an effort I could call her by her name. Even that exhausted me. My mind was so weak that I should have believed her, if she had declared herself to be a spirit seen in a dream, keeping watch over me in the wood.

Wiser than I was, she snatched up my hat, ran on before me, and was lost in the darkness.

An interval, an unendurable interval, passed. She returned, having filled my hat from the spring. But for the exquisite coolness of the water falling on my face, trickling down my throat, I should have lost my senses again. In a few minutes more, I could take that dear hand, and hold it to me as if I was holding to my life. We could only see each other obscurely, and in that very circumstance (as we confessed to each other afterwards) we found the needful composure before we could speak.

'Cristel! what does it mean?'

'Poison,' she answered. 'And *he* has suffered too.'

To my astonishment, there was no anger in her tone: she spoke of him as quietly as if she had been alluding to an innocent man.

'Do you mean that he has been at death's door, like me?'

'Yes, thank God – or I should never have found you here. Poor old Gloody came to us, in search of help. 'My master's in a swoon, and I can't bring him to.' Directly I heard that, I remembered that you had drunk what he had drunk. What had happened to him, must have happened to you. Don't ask me how long it was before I found you, and what I felt when I did find you. I do so want to enjoy my happiness! Only let me see you safely home, and I ask no more.'

She helped me to rise, with the encouraging words which she might have used to a child. She put my arm in hers, and led me carefully along through the wood, as if I had been an old man.

Cristel had saved my life – but she would hear of no allusion to it. She knew how the poisoner had plotted to get rid of me – but nothing that I could say induced her to tell me how she had made the discovery. In view of Trimley Deen, my guardian angel dropped my arm.

'Go on,' she said, 'and let me see the servant let you in, before I run home.'

If she had not been once more wiser than I was, I should have taken her with me to the house; I should have positively refused to let her go back by herself. Nothing that I could say or do had the slightest effect on her resolution. Does the man live who could have taken leave of her calmly, in my place? She tore herself away from me, with a sigh of bitterness that was dreadful to hear.

'Oh, my darling,' I said, 'do I distress you?'

'Horribly,' she answered; 'but you are not to blame.'

Those were her farewell words. I called after her. I tried to follow her. She was lost to me in the darkness.

CHAPTER XIV

GLOODY SETTLES THE ACCOUNT

A night of fever; a night, when I did slumber for a few minutes, of horrid dreams – this was what I might have expected, and this is what really happened. The fresh morning air, flowing through my open window, cooled and composed me; the mercy of sleep found me. When I woke, and looked at my watch, I was a new man. The hour was noon.

I rang my bell. The servant announced that a man was waiting to see me. 'The same man, sir, who was found in the garden, looking at your flowers.' I at once gave directions to have him shown up to my bedroom. The delay of dressing was more than I had patience to encounter. Unless I was completely mistaken, here was the very person whom I wanted to enlighten me.

Gloody showed himself at the door, with a face ominously wretched, as well as ugly. I instantly thought of Cristel.

'If you bring me bad news,' I said, 'don't keep me waiting for it.'

'It's nothing that need trouble You, sir. I'm dismissed from my master's service – that's all.'

It was plainly not 'all'. Relieved even by that guarded reply, I pointed to a chair by the bedside.

'Do you believe that I mean well by you?' I asked.

'I do, sir, with all my heart.'

'Then sit down, Gloody, and make a clean breast of it.'

He lifted his enormous fist, by way of emphasizing his answer.

'I was within a hair's breadth, sir, of striking him. If I hadn't kept my temper, I might have killed him.'

'What did he do?'

'Flew into a furious rage. I don't complain of that; I daresay
I deserved it. Please to excuse my getting up again. I can't look
you in the face, and tell you of it.' He walked away to the
window. 'Even a poor devil, like me, does sometimes feel it
when he is insulted. Mr Roylake, he kicked me. Say no more
about it, sir! I would never have mentioned it, if I hadn't had
something else to tell you; only I don't know how.' In his
difficulty, he came back to my bedside. 'Look here, sir! What I
say is – that kick has wiped out the debt of thanks I owe him.
Yes. I say the account between us two is settled now, on both
sides. In two words, sir, if you mean to charge him before the
magistrates with attempting your life, I'll take my Bible oath
he did attempt it, and you may call me as your witness. There!
Now it's out.'

What his master had no doubt inferred, was what I saw
plainly too. Cristel had saved my life, and had been directed
how to do it by the poor fellow who had suffered in my cause.

'We will wait a little before we talk of setting the law in
force,' I said. 'In the meantime, Gloody, I want you to tell me
what you would tell the magistrate if I called you as a witness.'

He considered a little. 'The magistrate would put questions
to me – wouldn't he, sir? Very good. You put questions to
me, and I'll answer them to the best of my ability.'

The investigation that followed was far too long and too
wearisome to be related here. If I give the substance of it, I
shall have done enough.

Sometimes when he was awake, and supposed that he was
alone – sometimes when he was asleep and dreaming – The
Cur had betrayed himself. (It was a paltry vengeance, I own,
to gratify a malicious pleasure – as I did now – in thinking of
him and speaking of him by the degrading name which his
morbid humility had suggested. But are the demands of a
man's dignity always paid in the ready money of prompt
submission?) Anyway, it appeared that Gloody had heard
enough, in the sleeping moments and the solitary moments
of his master, to give him some idea of the jealous hatred
with which The Cur regarded me. He had done his best to
warn me, without actually betraying the man who had
rescued him from starvation or the workhouse – and he had
failed.

But his resolution to do me good service, in return for my kindness to him, far from being shaken, was confirmed by circumstances.

When his master returned to the chemical studies which have been already mentioned, Gloody was employed as assistant, to the extent of his limited capacity for making himself useful. He had no reason to suppose that I was the object of any of the experiments, until the day before the tea-party. Then, he saw the dog enticed into the new cottage, and apparently killed by the administration of poison of some sort. After an interval, a dose of another kind was poured down the poor creature's throat, and he began to revive. A lapse of a quarter of an hour followed; the last dose was repeated; and the dog soon sprang to his feet again, as lively as ever. Gloody was thereupon told to set the animal free; and was informed at the same time that he would be instantly dismissed, if he mentioned to any living creature what he had just seen.

By what process he arrived at the suspicion that my safety might be threatened, by the experiment on the dog, he was entirely unable to explain.

'It was borne in on my mind, sir; and that's all I can tell you,' he said. 'I didn't dare speak to you about it; you wouldn't have believed me. Or, if you did believe me, you might have sent for the police. The one way of putting a stop to murdering mischief (if murdering mischief it might be) was to trust Miss Cristel. That she was fond of you – I don't mean any offence, sir – I pretty well guessed. That she was true as steel, and not easily frightened, I didn't need to guess; I knew it.'

Gloody had done his best to prepare Cristel for the terrible confidence which he had determined to repose in her, and had not succeeded. What the poor girl must have suffered, I could but too readily understand, on recalling the startling changes in her look and manner when we met at the river-margin of the wood. She was pledged to secrecy, under penalty of ruining the man who was trying to save me; and to her presence of mind was trusted the whole responsibility of preserving my life. What a situation for a girl of eighteen!

'We made it out between us, sir, in two ways,' Gloody proceeded. 'First and foremost, she was to invite herself to tea. And, being at the table, she was to watch my master. Whatever she saw him drink, she was to insist on your drinking it too. You heard me ask leave to make the tea?'

'Yes.'

'Well, that was one of the signals agreed on between us. When he sent me away, we were certain of what he had it in his mind to do.'

'And when you looked at Miss Cristel, and she was too busy with her brooch to notice you, was that another signal?'

'It was, sir. When she handled her silver ornament, she told me that I might depend on her to forget nothing, and to be afraid of nothing.'

I remembered the quiet firmness in her face, after the prayer that she had said in her own room. Her steady resolution no longer surprised me.

'Did you wonder, sir, what possessed her,' Gloody went on, 'when she burst out singing? That was a signal to me. We wanted him out of our way, while you were made to drink what he had drunk out of the jug.'

'How did you know that he would not drink the whole contents of the jug?'

'You forget, sir, that I had seen the dog revived by two doses, given with a space of time between them.'

I ought to have remembered this, after what he had already told me. My intelligence brightened a little as I went on.

'And your accident in the next room was planned, of course?' I said. 'Do you think he saw through it? I should say, No; judging by his looks. He turned pale when he felt the floor shaken by your fall. For once in a way, he was honest – honestly frightened.'

'I noticed the same thing, sir, when he picked me up, off the floor. A man who can change his complexion, at will, is a man we hav'n't heard of yet, Mr Roylake.'

I had been dressing for some time past; longing to see Cristel, it is needless to say.

'Is there anything more,' I asked, 'that I ought to know?'

'Only one thing, Mr Roylake, that I can think of,' Gloody replied. 'I'm afraid it's Miss Cristel's turn next.'

'What do you mean?'

'While the deaf man lodges at the cottage, he means mischief, and his eye is on Miss Cristel. Early this morning, sir, I happened to be at the boat-house. Somebody (I leave you to guess who it is) has stolen the oars.'

I was dressed by this time, and so eager to get to the cottage, that I had already opened my door. What I had just heard brought me back into the room. As a matter of course, we both suspected the same person of stealing the oars. Had we any proof to justify us?

Gloody at once acknowledged that we had no proof. 'I happened to look at the boat,' he said, 'and I missed the oars. Oh, yes; I searched the boat-house. No oars! no oars!'

'And nothing more that you have forgotten, and ought to tell me?'

'Nothing, sir.'

I left Gloody to wait my return; being careful to place him under the protection of the upper servants – who would see that he was treated with respect by the household generally.

CHAPTER XV

THE MILLER'S HOSPITALITY

On the way to Toller's cottage, my fears for Cristel weighed heavily on my mind.

That the man who had tried to poison me was capable of committing any other outrage, provided he saw a prospect of escaping with impunity, no sane person could hesitate to conclude. But the cause of my alarm was not to be traced to this conviction. It was a doubt that made me tremble.

After what I had myself seen, and what Gloody had told me, could I hope to match my penetration, or the penetration of any person about me whom I could trust, against the fathomless cunning, the Satanic wickedness, of the villain who was still an inmate with Cristel, under her father's roof?

I have spoken of his fathomless cunning, and his Satanic wickedness. The manner in which the crime had been prepared and carried out would justify stronger expressions still. Such was the deliberate opinion of the lawyer whom I privately consulted, under circumstances still to be related.

'Let us arrive at a just appreciation of the dangerous scoundrel whom we have to deal with,' this gentleman said. 'His preliminary experiment with the dog; his resolution to make suspicion an impossibility, by drinking from the same tea which he had made ready for you; his skilled preparation of an antidote, the colour of which might court appearances by imitating water – are there many poisoners clever enough to provide themselves beforehand with such a defence as this? How are you to set the circumstances in their true light, on your side? You may say that you threw out the calculations, on which he had relied for securing his own safety, by drinking his second dose of the antidote while he was out of the room; and you can appeal to the fainting-fits from which

100

you and he suffered on the same evening, as a proof that the action of the poison was partially successful; in your case and in his, because you and he were insufficiently protected by half doses only of the antidote. A bench of Jesuits would understand these refinements. A bench of British magistrates would look at each other, and say: Where is the medical evidence? No, Mr Roylake, we must wait. You can't even turn him out of the cottage before he has had the customary notice to quit. The one thing to take care of – in case some other suspicions of ours turn out to be well founded – is that our man shall not give us the slip. One of my clerks, and one of your game-keepers shall keep watch on his lodgings, turn and turn about, till his time is up. Go where he may after that, he shall not escape us.'

I may now take up the chain of events again.

On reaching Toller's cottage, I was distressed (but hardly surprised) to hear that Cristel, exhausted after a wakeful night, still kept her bed, in the hope of getting some sleep. I was so anxious to know if she was at rest, that her father went upstairs to look at her.

I followed him – and saw Ponto watching on the mat outside her door. Did this indicate a wise distrust of The Cur? 'A guardian I can trust, sir,' the old man whispered, 'while I'm at the mill.'

He looked into Cristel's room, and permitted me to look over his shoulder. My poor darling was peacefully asleep. Judging by the miller's manner, which was as cool and composed as usual, I gathered that Cristel had wisely kept him in ignorance of what had happened on the previous evening.

The inquiry which I had next in my mind was forestalled by old Toller.

'Our deaf-devil, Mr Gerard, has done a thing this morning which puzzles me,' he began; 'and I should like to hear what you think of it. For the first time since we have had him here, he has opened his door to a visitor. And – what a surprise for you! – it's the other devil with the hat and feather who got at my Cristy, and made her cry.'

That this meeting would be only too likely to happen, in due course of time, I had never doubted. That it had happened, now, confirmed me in my resolution to keep guard over Cristel at the cottage, till The Cur left it.

I asked, of course, how those two enemies of mine had first seen each other.

'She was just going to knock at our door, Mr Gerard, when she happened to look up. There he was, airing himself at his window as usual. Do you think she was too much staggered at the sight of him to speak? At any rate, he got the start of her. 'Wait till I come down,' says he – and there he was, almost as soon as he said it. They went into his place together; and for best part of an hour they were in each other's company. Every man has his failings; I don't deny that I'm a little inquisitive by nature. Between ourselves, I got under the open window and listened. At a great disadvantage, I needn't tell you; for she was obliged to write what she had to say. But *he* talked. I was too late for the cream of it; I only heard him wish her good-bye. 'If your ladyship telegraphs this morning,' says he, 'when will the man come to me?' Now what do you say to that?'

'More than I have time to say now, Mr Toller. Can you find me a messenger to take a note to Trimley Deen?'

'We have no messengers in this lonesome place, sir.'

'Very well. Then I must take my own message. You will see me again, as soon as I can get back.'

Mr Toller's ready curiosity was roused in a moment.

'Perhaps, you wish to have a look at the repairs?' he suggested in his most insinuating manner.

'I wish to see what her ladyship's telegram brings forth,' I said; 'and I mean to be here when "the man" arrives.'

My venerable tenant was delighted. 'Turn him inside out, sir, and get at his secrets. I'll help you.'

Returning to Trimley Deen, I ordered the pony-chaise to be got ready, and a small portmanteau to be packed – speaking in the hall. The sound of my voice brought Mrs Roylake out of the morning-room. She was followed by Lady Rachel. If I could only have heard their private conference, I should have seen the dangerous side of The Cur's character under a new aspect.

'Gerard!' cried my stepmother, 'what did I hear just now? You can't be going back to Germany!'

'Certainly not,' I answered.

'Going to stay with some friends perhaps?' Lady Rachel suggested. 'I wonder whether I know them?'

It was spitefully done – but, in respect of tone and manner, done to perfection.

The pony-chaise drew up at the door. This was another of the rare occasions in my life on which I acted discreetly. It was necessary for me to say something. I said, 'Good morning.'

Nothing had happened at the cottage, during the interval of my absence. Clever as he was, old Toller had never suspected that I should return to him (with luggage!) in the character of a self-invited guest. His jaw dropped, and his wicked little eyes appealed to the sky. Merciful Providence! what have I done to deserve this? There, as I read him, was the thought in the miller's mind, expressed in my best English.

'Have you got a spare bed in the house?' I asked.

Mr Toller forgot the respect due to the person who could stop the repairs at a moment's notice. He answered in the tone of a man who had been grossly insulted: 'No!'

But for the anxieties that oppressed me, I should have only perceived the humorous side of old Toller's outbreak of temper. He had chosen his time badly, and he got a serious reply.

'Understand this,' I said: 'either you receive me civilly – or you make up your mind to find a flour-mill on some other property than mine.'

This had its effect. The miller's servility more than equalled his insolence. With profuse apologies, he offered me his own bedroom. I preferred a large old-fashioned armchair which stood in a corner of the kitchen. Listening in a state of profound bewilderment – longing to put inquisitive questions, and afraid to do so – Toller silently appealed to my compassion. I had nothing to conceal; I mentioned my motive. Without intending it, I had wounded him in one of his most tender places; the place occupied by his good opinion of himself. He said with sulky submission:

'Much obliged, Mr Gerard. My girl is safe under *my* protection. Leave it to me, sir – leave it to me.'

I had just reminded old Toller of his age, and of the infirmities which age brings with it, when his daughter – pale and languid, with signs of recent tears in her eyes – entered the kitchen. When I approached her, she trembled and drew back; apparently designing to leave the room. Her father stopped her. 'Mr Gerard has something to tell you,' he said. 'I'm off to the mill.' He took up his hat, and left us.

Submitting sadly, she let me take her in my arms, and try to cheer her. But when I alluded to what I owed to her admirable devotion and courage, she entreated me to be silent. 'Don't bring it all back!' she cried, shuddering at the remembrances which I had awakened. 'Father said you had something to tell me. What is it?'

I repeated (in language more gentle and more considerate) what I had already said to her father. She took my hand, and kissed it gratefully. 'You have your mother's face, and your mother's heart,' she said; 'you are always good, you are never selfish. But it mustn't be. How can I let you suffer the discomfort of staying here? Indeed, I am in no danger; you are alarming yourself without a cause.'

'How can you be sure of that?' I asked.

She looked reluctantly at the door of communication.

'Must I speak of him?'

'Only to tell me,' I pleaded, 'whether you have seen him since last night.'

She had both seen him and heard from him, on reaching home. 'He opened that door,' she told me, 'and threw on the floor one of the leaves out of his book. After doing that, he relieved me from the sight of him.'

'Show me the leaf, Cristel.'

'Father has got it. I thought he was asleep in the armchair. He snatched it out of my hand. It isn't worth reading.'

She turned pale, nevertheless, when she replied in those terms. I could see that I was disturbing her, when I asked if she remembered what The Cur had written. But our position was far too serious to be trifled with. 'I suppose he threatened you?' I said, trying to lead her on. 'What did he say?'

'He said, if any attempt was made to remove me out of his reach, after what had happened that evening, my father would find him on the watch day and night, and would regret it to the end of his life. The wretch thinks me cruel enough to have told my father of the horrors we went through! You know that he has dismissed his poor old servant? Was I wrong in advising Gloody to go to you?'

'You were quite right. He is at my house – and I should like to keep him at Trimley Deen; but I am afraid he and the other servants might not get on well together?'

'Will you let him come here?'

She spoke earnestly; reminding me that I had thought it wrong to leave her father, at his age, without someone to help him.

'If an accident separated me from him,' she went on, 'he would be left alone in this wretched place.'

'What accident are you thinking of?' I asked. 'Is there something going on, Cristel, that I don't know of?'

Had I startled her? or had I offended her?

'Can we tell what may or may not happen to us, in the time to come?' she asked abruptly. I don't like to think of my father being left without a creature to take care of him. Gloody is so good and so true; and they always get on well together. If you have nothing better in view for him——?'

'My dear, I have nothing half so good in view; and Gloody, I am sure, will think so too.' I privately resolved to insure a favourable reception for the poor fellow, by making him the miller's partner. Bank notes in Toller's pocket! What a place reserved for Gloody in Toller's estimation!

But I confess that Cristel's allusion to a possible accident rather oppressed my mind, situated as we were at that time. What we talked of next has slipped from my memory. I only recollect that she made an excuse to go back to her room, and that nothing I could say or do availed to restore her customary cheerfulness.

As the twilight was beginning to fade, we heard the sound of a carriage. The new man had arrived in a fly from the station. Before bedtime, he made his appearance in the kitchen, to receive the domestic instructions of which a stranger stood in need. A quiet man and a civil man: even my prejudiced examination could discover nothing in him that looked suspicious. I saw a well-trained servant – and I saw nothing more.

Old Toller made a last attempt to persuade me that it was not worth a gentleman's while to accept his hospitality, and

found me immovable. I was equally obstinate when Cristel asked
leave to make up a bed for me in the counting-house at the mill.

With the purpose that I had in view, if I accepted her
proposal I might as well have been at Trimley Deen.

Left alone, I placed the armchair and another chair for my
feet, across the door of communication. That done, I examined a little door behind the stairs (used I believe for domestic
purposes) which opened on a narrow pathway, running along
the river-side of the house. It was properly locked. I have only
to add that nothing happened during the night.

The next day showed no alteration for the better, in Cristel.
She made an excuse when I proposed to take her out with me
for a walk. Her father's business kept him away from the
cottage, and thus gave me many opportunities of speaking to
her in private. I was so uneasy, or so reckless – I hardly know
which – that I no longer left it to be merely inferred that I had
resolved to propose marriage to her.

'My sweet girl, you are so wretched, and so unlike yourself,
in this place, that I entreat you to leave it. Come with me to
London, and let me make you safe and happy as my wife.'

'Oh, Mr Roylake!'

'Why do you call me, "Mr Roylake"? Have I done anything
to offend you? There seems to be some estrangement between
us. Do you believe that I love You?'

'I wish I could doubt it!' she answered.

'Why?'

'You know why.'

'Cristel! Have I made some dreadful mistake? The truth! I
want the truth! Do you love me?'

A low cry of misery burst from her. Was she mastered by
love, or by despair? She threw herself on my breast. I kissed
her. She murmured, 'Oh don't tempt me! Don't tempt me!'
Again and again, I kissed her. 'Ah,' I broke out, in the ecstasy
of my sense of relief, 'I know that you love me, now!'

'Yes,' she said, simply and sadly, 'I do love you.'

My selfish passion asked for more even than this.

'Prove it by being my wife,' I answered.

She put me back from her, firmly and gently.

'I will prove it, Gerard, by not letting you disgrace
yourself.'

With those horrible words – put into her mouth, beyond all doubt by the woman who had interfered between us – she left me. The long hours of the day passed: I saw her no more.

People who are unable to imagine what I suffered, are not the people to whom I now address myself. After all the years that have passed – after age and contact with the world have hardened me – it is still a trial to my self-control to look back to that day. Events I can remember with composure. To events, therefore, let me return.

No communication of any sort reached us from The Cur. Towards evening, I saw him pacing up and down on the road before the cottage, and speaking to his new servant. The man (listening attentively) had the master's book of leaves in his hand, and wrote in it from time to time as replies were wanted from him. He was probably receiving instructions. The Cur's discretion was a bad sign. I should have felt more at ease, if he had tried to annoy Cristel, or to insult me.

Towards bedtime, old Toller's sense of hospitality exhibited marked improvement. He was honoured and happy to have me under his poor roof – a roof, by the way, which was also in need of repairs – but he protested against my encountering the needless hardship of sleeping in a chair, when a bed could be set up for me in the counting-house. 'Not what you're used to, Mr Gerard. Empty barrels, and samples of flour, and account-books smelling strong of leather, instead of velvet curtains and painted ceilings; but better than a chair, sir – better than a chair!'

I was as obstinate as ever. With thanks, I insisted on the chair.

Feverish, anxious, oppressed in my breathing – with nerves unstrung, as a doctor would have put it – I disturbed the order of the household towards twelve o'clock by interfering with old Toller in the act of locking up the house-door.

'Let me get a breath of fresh air,' I said to him, 'or there will be no sleep for me to-night.'

He opened the door with a resignation to circumstances, so exemplary that it claimed some return. I promised to be back in a quarter of an hour. Old Toller stifled a yawn. 'I call that truly considerate,' he said – and stifled another yawn. Dear old man!

Stepping into the road, I first examined The Cur's part of the cottage. Not a sound was audible inside; not a creature was visible outside. The usual dim light was burning behind the window that looked out on the road. Nothing, absolutely nothing, that was suspicious could I either hear or see.

I walked on, by what we called the upper bank of the river; leading from the village of Kylam. The night was cloudy and close. Now the moonlight reached the earth at intervals; now again it was veiled in darkness. The trees, at this part of the wood, so encroached on the bank of the stream as considerably to narrow and darken the path. Seeing a possibility of walking into the river if I went on much farther, I turned back again in the more open direction of Kylam, and kept on briskly (as I reckon) for about five minutes more.

I had just stopped to look at my watch, when I saw something dark floating towards me, urged by the slow current of the river. As it came nearer, I thought I recognized the mill-boat.

It was one of the dark intervals when the moon was overcast. I was sufficiently interested to follow the boat, on the chance that a return of the moonlight might show me who could possibly be in it. After no very long interval, the yellow light for which I was waiting poured through the lifting clouds.

The mill-boat, beyond all doubt – and nobody in it! The empty inside of the boat was perfectly visible to me. Even if I had felt inclined to do so, it would have been useless to jump into the water and swim to the boat. There were no oars in it, and therefore no means of taking it back to the mill. The one thing I could do was to run to old Toller and tell him that his boat was adrift.

On my way to the cottage, I thought I heard a sound like the shutting of a door. I was probably mistaken. In expectation of my return, the door was secured by the latch only; and the miller, looking out of his bedroom window, said: 'Don't forget to lock it, sir; the key's inside.'

I followed my instructions, and ascended the stairs. Surprised to hear me in that part of the house, he came out on the landing in his nightgown.

'What is it?' he asked.

'Nothing very serious,' I said. 'The boat's adrift. I suppose it will run on shore somewhere.'

'It will do that, Mr Gerard; everybody along the river knows the boat.' He held up his lean trembling hand. 'Old fingers don't always tie fast knots.'

He went back into his bed. It was opposite the window; and the window, being at the side of the old cottage, looked out on the great open space above the river. When the moonlight appeared, it shone straight into his eyes. I offered to pull down the blind.

'Thank you kindly, sir; please to let it be. I wake often in the night, and I like to see the heavens when I open my eyes.'

Something touched me behind: it was the dog. Like his noble and beautiful race, Ponto knew his friends. He licked my hand, and then he walked out through the bedroom door. Instead of taking his usual place, on the mat before Cristel's room, he smelt for a moment under the door – whined softly – and walked up and down the landing.

'What's the matter with the dog?' I asked.

'Restless to–night,' said old Toller. 'Dogs *are* restless sometimes. Lie down!' he called through the doorway.

The dog obeyed, but only for a moment. He whined at the door again – and then, once more, he walked up and down the landing.

I went to the bedside. The old man was just going to sleep. I shook him by the shoulder.

'There's something wrong,' I said. 'Come out and look at Ponto.'

He grumbled – but he came out. 'Better get the whip,' he said.

'Before you do that,' I answered, 'knock at your daughter's door.'

'And wake her?' he asked in amazement.

I knocked at the door myself. There was no reply. I knocked again, with the same result.

'Open the door,' I said, 'or I will do it myself.'

He obeyed me. The room was empty; and the bed had not been slept in.

Standing helpless on the threshold of the door, I looked into the empty room; hearing nothing but my heart thumping heavily, seeing nothing but the bed with the clothes on it undisturbed.

The sudden growling of the dog shook me back (if I may say so) into the possession of myself. He was looking through the balusters that guarded the landing. The head of a man appeared, slowly ascending the stairs. Acting mechanically, I held the dog back. Thinking mechanically, I waited for the man. The face of the new servant showed itself. The dog frightened him: he spoke in tones that trembled, standing still on the stairs.

'My master has sent me, sir——'

A voice below interrupted him. 'Come back,' I heard The Cur say; 'I'll do it myself. Toller! where is Toller?'

The enraged dog, barking furiously, struggled to get away from me. I dragged him – the good honest creature who was incapable of concealments and treacheries! – into his master's room. In the moment before I closed the door again, I saw Toller down on his knees with his arms laid helplessly on the window-sill, staring up at the sky as if he had gone mad. There was no time for questions; I drove poor Ponto back into the room, and shut the door.

On the landing, I found myself face to face with The Cur.

'*You!*' he said.

I lifted my hand. The servant ran between us. 'For God's sake, control yourself, sir! We mean no harm. It's only to tell Mr Toller that his boat is missing.'

'Mr Toller knows it already,' I said. 'No honest man would touch your master if he could help it. I warn him to go; and I make him understand me by a sign.' I pointed down the stairs, and turned my head to look at him.

He was no longer before me. His face, hideously distorted by rage and terror, showed itself at the door of Cristel's empty room. He rushed out on me; his voice rose to the detestable screech which I had heard once already.

'Where have you hidden her? Give her back to me – or you die.' He drew a pistol out of the breast-pocket of his coat. I seized the weapon by the barrel, and snatched it away from him. As the charge exploded harmlessly between us, I struck him on the head with the butt-end of the pistol. He dropped on the landing.

The door of Toller's room opened behind me. He stood speechless; the report of the pistol had terrified him. In the instant when I looked at the old man, I saw, through the window of his room, a rocket soar into the sky, from behind the promontory between us and Kylam.

Some cry of surprise must, I suppose, have escaped me. Toller suddenly looked round towards the window, just as the last fiery particles of the rocket were floating slowly downwards against the black clouds.

I had barely time enough to see this, before a trembling hand was laid on my shoulder, from behind. The servant, white with terror, pointed to his master.

'Have you killed him?' the man said.

The same question must have been in the mind of the dog. He was quiet now. Doubtfully, reluctantly, he was smelling at the prostrate human creature. I knelt down, and put my hand on the wretch's heart. Ponto, finding us both on a level together, gave me the dog's kiss; I returned the caress with my free hand. The servant saw me, with my attention divided in this way between the animal and the man.

'Damn it, sir,' he burst out indignantly, 'isn't a Christian of more importance than a dog?'

A Christian! – but I was in no humour to waste words. 'Are you strong enough to carry him to his own side of the house?' I asked.

'I won't touch him, if he's dead!'

'He is *not* dead. Take him away!'

All this time my mind was pre-occupied by the extraordinary appearance of the rocket, rising from the neighbourhood of a lonely little village between midnight and one in the morning. How I connected that mysterious signal with a possibility of tracing Cristel, it is useless to inquire. That was the thought in me, when I led my lost darling's father back to his room. Without stopping to explain myself, I reminded him that the cottage was quiet again, and told him to wait my return.

In the kitchen, I overtook the servant and his burden. The door of communication (by which they had entered) was still open.

'Lock that door,' I said.

'Lock it yourself,' he answered; 'I'll have nothing to do with this business.' He passed through the doorway, and along the passage, and ascended his master's stairs.

It struck me directly that the man had suggested a sure way of protecting Toller, during my absence. The miller's own door was already secured; I took the key, so as to be able to let myself in again – then passed through the door of communication – fastened it – and put the key in my pocket. The third door, by which The Cur entered his lodgings, was of course at my disposal. I had just closed it, when I discovered that I had a companion. Ponto had followed me.

I felt at once that the dog's superior powers of divination might be of use, on such an errand as mine was. We set out together for Kylam.

Wildly hurried – without any fixed idea in my mind – I ran to Kylam, for the greater part of the way. It was now very dark. On a sandy creek, below the village, I came in contact with something solid enough to hurt me for the moment. It was the stranded boat.

A smoker generally has matches about him. Helped by my little short-lived lights, I examined the interior of the boat. There was absolutely nothing in it but a strip of old tarpaulin – used, as I guessed, to protect the boat, or something that it carried, in rainy weather.

The village population had long since been in bed. Silence and darkness mercilessly defied me to discover anything. For a while I waited, encouraging the dog to circle round me and exercise his sense of smell. Any suspicious person or object he would have certainly discovered. Nothing – not even the fallen stick of the rocket – rewarded our patience. Determined to leave nothing untried, I groped, rather than found, my way to the village ale house, and succeeded at last in rousing the landlord. He hailed me from the window (naturally enough) in no friendly voice. I called out my name. Within my own little limits, it was the name of a celebrated person. The landlord opened his door directly; eager to answer my questions if he could do it. Nothing in the least out of the common way had happened at Kylam. No strangers had been seen in, or near, the place. The stranded boat had not been discovered; and the crashing flight of the rocket into the air had failed to disturb the soundly-sleeping villagers.

On my melancholy way back, fatigue of body – and, far worse, fatigue of mind – forced me to take a few minutes' rest.

The dimly-flowing river was at my feet; the river on which I had seen Cristel again, for the first time since we were children. Thus far, the dreadful loss of her had been a calamity, held away from me in some degree by events which had imperatively taken possession of my mind. In the darkness and the stillness, the misery of having lost her was free to crush me. My head dropped on the neck of the dog, nestling close at my side. 'Oh, Ponto!' I said to him, 'she's gone!' Nobody could see me; nobody could despise me – I burst out crying.

CHAPTER XVI

BRIBERY AND CORRUPTION

Twice, I looked into Toller's room during the remainder of the night, and found him sleeping. When the sun rose, I could endure the delay no longer. I woke him.

'What is it?' he asked peevishly.

'You must be the last person who saw Cristel,' I answered. 'I want to know all that you can tell me.'

His anger completely mastered him; he burst out with a furious reply.

'It's you two – you my landlord, and him my lodger – who have driven Cristy away from her home. She said she would go, and she *has* gone. Get out of my place, sir! You ought to be ashamed to look at me.'

It was useless to reason with him, and it was of vital importance to lose no time in instituting a search. After the reception I had met with, I took care to restore the key of the door leading into the new cottage, before I left him. It was his key; and the poor distracted old man might charge me with taking away his property next.

As I set forth on my way home, I found the new man-servant on the look-out.

His first words showed that he was acting under orders. He asked if I had found the young lady; and he next informed me that his master had revived some hours since, and 'bore no malice'. This outrageous assertion suddenly fired me with suspicion. I believed that The Cur had been acting a part when he threatened me with his pistol, and that he was answerable for the disappearance of Cristel. My first impulse now was to get the help of a lawyer.

The men at my stables were just stirring when I got home. In ten minutes more, I was driving to our town.

The substance of the professional opinion which I received has been already stated in these pages.

One among my answers to the many questions which my legal adviser put to me led him to a conclusion that made my heart ache. He was of opinion that my brief absence, while I was taking that fatal 'breath of air' on the banks of the river, had offered to Cristel her opportunity of getting away without discovery. 'Her old father,' the lawyer said, 'was no doubt in his bed, and you yourself found nobody watching, in the neighbourhood of the cottage.'

'Employ me in some way!' I burst out. 'I can't endure my life, if I'm not helping to trace Cristel.'

He was most kind. 'I understand,' he said. 'Try what you can get those two ladies to tell you – and you may help us materially.'

Mrs Roylake was nearest to me. I appealed to her womanly sympathies, and was answered by tears. I made another attempt; I said I was willing to believe that she meant well, and that I should be sorry to offend her. She got up, and indignantly left the room.

I went to Lady Rachel next.

She was at home, but the servant returned to me with an excuse: her ladyship was particularly engaged. I sent a message upstairs, asking when I might hope to be received. The servant was charged with the delivery of another excuse: her ladyship would write. After waiting at home for hours I was foolish enough to write, on my side; and (how could I help it?) to express myself strongly. The she-socialist's reply is easy to remember: 'Dear Mr Roylake, when you have recovered your temper, you will hear from me again.'

Even my stepmother gained by comparison with this.

To rest, and do nothing, was to exercise a control over myself of which I was perfectly incapable. I went back to the cottage. Having no hopeful prospect in any other quarter, I persisted in believing that Toller must have seen something or heard something that might either help me, or suggest an idea to my legal adviser.

On entering the kitchen, I found the door of communication wide open, and the new servant established in the large armchair.

'I'm waiting for my master, sir.'

He had got over his fright, and had recovered his temper. The respectful side of him was turned to me again.

'Your master is with Mr Toller?'

'Yes, sir.'

What I felt, amply justified the lawyer in having exacted a promise from me to keep carefully out of The Cur's presence. 'You might knock him on the head again, Mr Roylake, and might hit a little too hard next time.'

But I had an idea of my own. I said, as if speaking to myself: 'I would give a five pound note to know what is going on upstairs.'

'I shall be glad to earn it, sir,' the fellow said. 'If I make a clean breast of what I know already, and if I tell you to-morrow what I can find out – will it be worth the money?'

I began to feel degraded in my own estimation. But I nodded to him, for all that.

'I am the innocent cause, sir, of what happened last night,' he coolly resumed. 'We kept a look-out on the road and saw you, though you didn't see us. But my master never suspected you (for reasons which he kept to himself) of making use of the boat. I reminded him that one of us had better have an eye on the slip of pathway, between the cottage and the river. This led to his sending me to the boat-house – and you know what happened afterwards. My master, as I suppose, is pumping Mr Toller. That's all, sir, for to-night. When may I have the honour of expecting you to-morrow morning?'

I appointed an hour, and left the place.

As I entered the wood again, I found a man on the watch. He touched his hat, and said: 'I'm the clerk, sir. Your gamekeeper is wanted for his own duties to-night; he will relieve me in the morning.'

I went home with my mind in a ferment of doubt. If I could believe the servant, The Cur was as innocent of the abduction of Cristel as I was. But could I trust the servant?

The events of the next morning altered the whole complexion of affairs fatally for the worse.

Arriving at the cottage, I found a man prostrate on the road, dead drunk – and The Cur's servant looking at him.

'May I ask something?' the man said. 'Have you been having my master watched?'

'Yes.'

'Bad news, in that case, sir. Your man there is a drunken vagabond; and my master has gone to London by the first train.'

When I had recovered the shock, I denied, for the sake of my own credit, that the brute on the road could be a servant of mine.

'Why not, sir?'

'Do you think I should have been kept in ignorance of it, if my gamekeeper had been a drunkard? His fellow servants would have warned me.'

The man smiled. 'I'm afraid, sir, you don't know much about servants. It's a point of honour among us never to tell tales of each other to our masters.'

I began to wish that I had never left Germany. The one course to take now was to tell the lawyer what had happened. I turned away to get back, and drive at once to the town. The servant remembered, what I had forgotten – the five pound note.

'Wait and hear my report, sir,' he suggested.

The report informed me: First, that Mr Toller was at the mill, and had been there for some time past. Secondly: that The Cur had been alone, for a while, on Mr Toller's side of the cottage, in Mr Toller's absence – for what purpose his servant had not discovered. Thirdly: that The Cur had returned to his room in a hurry, and had packed a few things in his travelling-bag. Fourthly: that he had ordered the servant to follow, with his luggage, in a fly which he would send from the railway station, and to wait at the London terminus for further orders. Fifthly, and lastly: that it was impossible to say whether the drunkenness of the gamekeeper was due to his own habits, or to temptation privately offered by the very person whose movements he had been appointed to watch.

I paid the money. The man pocketed it, and paid me a compliment in return: 'I wish I was your servant, sir.'

CHAPTER XVII

UTTER FAILURE

My lawyer took a serious view of the disaster that had overtaken us. He would trust nobody but his head clerk to act in my interests, after the servant had been followed to the London terminus, and when it became a question of matching ourselves against the deadly cunning of the man who had escaped us.

Provided with money, and with a letter to the police authorities in London, the head clerk went to the station. I accompanied him to point out the servant (without being allowed to show myself), and then returned to wait for telegraphic information at the lawyer's office.

This was the first report transmitted by the telegram:

The Cur had been found waiting for his servant at the terminus; and the two had been easily followed to the railway hotel close by. The clerk had sent his letter of introduction to the police – had consulted with picked men who joined him at the hotel – had given the necessary instructions – and would return to us by the last train in the evening.

In two days, the second telegram arrived.

Our man had been traced to the Thames Yacht Club in Albemarle Street – had consulted a yachting list in the hall – and had then travelled to the Isle of Wight. There, he had made inquiries at the Squadron Yacht Club, and the Victoria Yacht Club – and had returned to London, and the railway hotel.

The third telegram announced the utter destruction of all our hopes. As far as Marseilles, The Cur had been followed successfully, and in that city the detective officers had lost sight of him.

My legal adviser insisted on having the men sent to him to explain themselves. Nothing came of it but one more repetition of an old discovery. When the detective police force encounters intelligence instead of stupidity, in seven cases out of ten the detective police force is beaten.

There were still two persons at our disposal. Lady Rachel might help us, as I believed, if she chose to do it. As for old Toller, I suggested (on reflection) that the lawyer should examine him. The lawyer declined to waste any more of my money. I called again on Lady Rachel. This time, I was let in. I found the noble lady smoking a cigarette and reading a French novel.

'This is going to be a disagreeable interview,' she said. 'Let us get it over, Mr Roylake, as soon as possible. Tell me what you want – and speak as freely as if you were in the company of a man.'

I obeyed her to the letter; and I got these replies:

'Yes; I did have a talk, in your best interests, with Miss Toller. She is as sensible as she is charming, and as good as she is sensible. We entirely agreed that the sacrifice must be on her side; and that it was due to her own self-respect to prevent a gentleman of your rank from ruining himself by marrying a miller's daughter.'

The next reply was equally free from the smallest atom of sympathy on Lady Rachel's part.

'You are quite right – your deaf man was at his window when I went by. We recognized each other and had a long talk. If I remember correctly, he said you knew of his reasons for concealing his name. I gave my promise (being a matter of perfect indifference to me) to conceal it too. One thing led to another, and I discovered that you were his hated rival in the affections of Miss Toller. I proved worthy of his confidence in me. That is to say, I told him that Mrs Roylake and I would be only too glad, as representing your interests, if he succeeded in winning the young lady. I asked if he had any plans. He said one of his plans had failed. What it was, and how it had failed, he did not mention. I asked if he could devise nothing else. He said, 'Yes, if I was not a poor man.' In my place, you would have offered, as I did, to find the money if the plan was approved of. He produced some manuscript story of an abduction of a lady, which he had written to amuse himself. The point of it was that the lover successfully carried away the lady, by means of a boat, while the furious father's attention was absorbed in watching the high road. It seemed to me to be a new idea. 'If you think you can carry it out,' I said, 'send your estimate of expenses to me and Mrs Roylake, and we will subscribe.' We received the estimate. But the plan has failed, and the man is off. I am quite certain myself that Miss Toller has done what she promised to do. Wherever she may be now, she has sacrificed herself for your sake. When you have got over it, you will marry my sister. I wish you good morning.'

Between Lady Rachel's hard insolence, and Mrs Roylake's sentimental hypocrisy, I was in such a state of irritation that I left Trimley Deen the next morning, to find forgetfulness, as I rashly supposed, in the gay world of London.

I had been trying my experiment for something like three weeks, and was beginning to get heartily weary of it, when I received a letter from the lawyer.

Dear Sir, – Your odd tenant, old Mr Toller, has died suddenly of rupture of a blood-vessel on the brain, as the doctor thinks. There is to be an inquest, as I need hardly tell you. What do you say to having the report of the proceedings largely copied in the newspapers? If it catches his daughter's eye, important results may follow.

To speculate in this way on the impulse which might take its rise in my poor girl's grief – to surprise her, as it were, at her father's grave – revolted me. I directed the lawyer to take no steps whatever in the matter, and to pay the poor old fellow's funeral expenses, on my account. He had died intestate. The law took care of his money until his daughter appeared; and the mill, being my property, I gave to Toller's surviving partner – our good Gloody.

And what did I do next? I went away travelling; one of the wretchedest men who ever carried his misery with him to foreign countries. Go where I might on the continent of Europe, the dreadful idea pursued me that Cristel might be dead.

CHAPTER XVIII

THE MISTRESS OF TRIMLEY DEEN

Three weary months had passed, when a new idea was put into my head by an Englishman whom I met at Trieste. He advised turning my back on Europe, and trying the effect of scenes of life that would be new to me. I hired a vessel, and sailed out of the civilized world. When I next stood on *terra firma*, my feet were on the lovely beach of one of the Pacific Islands.

What I suffered I have not told yet, and do not design to tell. The bitterness of those days hid itself from view at the time – and shall keep its concealment still. Even if I could dwell on my sorrows with the eloquence of a practised writer, some obstinate inner reluctance would persist in holding me dumb.

More than a year had passed before I returned to Trimley Deen, and alarmed my stepmother by 'looking like a foreign sailor.'

The irregular nature of my later travels had made it impossible to forward the few letters that had arrived for me. They were neatly laid out on the library table.

The second letter that I took up bore the postmark of Genoa. I opened it, and discovered that the——

No! I cannot write of him by that mean name; and his own name is still unknown to me. Let me call him – and, oh, don't think that I am deceived again! – let me call him The Penitent.

The letter had been addressed to me from his deathbed, and had been written under dictation. It contained an extra-ordinary inclosure – a small torn fragment of paper with writing on it.

'Read the poor morsel that I send to you first' (the letter began). 'My time on earth is short; you will save me explanations which may be too much for my strength.'

On one side of the fragment, I found these words:

. . . cruise to the Mediterranean for my wife's health. If Cristel isn't afraid of passing some months at sea . . .

On the other side, there was a fragment of conclusion:

. . . thoroughly understand. All ready. Write word what night, and what . . . loving brother, Stephen Toller.

I instantly remembered the miller's rich brother; thinking of him for the first time since he had been in my mind for a moment, on the night of my meeting with Cristel. On the tenth page of this narrative Toller's brother will be found briefly alluded to in a few lines.

I returned eagerly to the letter. Thus it was continued:

That bit of torn paper I found under the bed, while I was secretly searching Mr Toller's room. I had previously suspected You. From my own examination of his face, when he refused to humour my deafness by writing what I asked him to tell me, I suspected Mr Toller next. You will see in the fragment, what I saw – that Toller the brother had a yacht, and was going to the Mediterranean; and that Toller the miller had written, asking him to favour Cristel's escape. The rest, Cristel herself can tell you.

I know you had me followed. At Marseilles, I got tired of it, and gave your men the slip. At every port in the Mediterranean I inquired for the yacht, and heard nothing of her. They must have changed their minds on board, and gone somewhere else. I refer you to Cristel again.

Arrived at Genoa, on my way back to England, I met with a skilled Italian surgeon. He declared that he could restore my hearing – but he warned me that I was in a weak state of health, and he refused to answer for the result of the operation. Without hesitating for a moment, I told him to operate. I would have given fifty lives for one exquisite week of perfect hearing. I have had three weeks of perfect hearing. Otherwise, I have had a life of enjoyment before I die.

It is useless to ask your pardon. My conduct was too infamous for that. Will you remember the family taint, developed by a deaf man's isolation among his fellow-creatures? But I had some days when my mother's sweet nature tried to make itself felt in me, and did not wholly fail. I am going to my mother now: her spirit has been with me ever since my hearing was restored; her spirit said to me last night: 'Atone, my son! Give the man whom you have wronged, the woman whom he loves.' I had found out the uncle's address in England (which I now enclose) at one of the Yacht Clubs. I had intended to go to the house, and welcome her on her return. You must go instead of me; you will see that lovely face when I am in my grave. Good-bye, Roylake. The cold hand that touches us all, sooner or later, is very near to me. Be merciful to the next scoundrel you meet, for the sake of The Cur.

I say there *was* good in that suffering man; and I thank God I was not quite wrong about him after all.

Arriving at Mr Stephen Toller's country seat, by the earliest train that would take me there, I found a last trial of endurance in store for me. Cristel was away with her uncle, visiting some friends.

Cristel's aunt received me with kindness which I can never forget. 'We have noticed lately that Cristel was in depressed spirits; no uncommon thing,' Mrs Stephen Toller continued, looking at me with a gentle smile, 'since a parting which I know you must have felt deeply too. No, Mr Roylake, she is not engaged to be married – and she will never be married, unless you forgive her. Ah, you forgive her because you love her! She thought of writing to tell you her motives, when she visited her father's grave on our return to England. But I was unable to obtain your address. Perhaps, I may speak for her now?'

I knew how Lady Rachel's interference had appealed to Cristel's sense of duty and sense of self-respect; I had heard from her own lips that she distrusted herself, if she allowed me to press her. But she had successfully concealed from me the terror with which she regarded her rejected lover, and the influence over her which her father had exercised. Always mindful of his own interests, the miller knew that he would be the person blamed if he allowed his daughter to marry me. 'They will say I did it, with an eye to my son-in-law's money; and gentlefolks may ruin a man who lives by selling flour.' That was how he expressed himself in a letter to his brother.

The whole of the correspondence was shown to me by Mrs Stephen Toller.

After alluding to his wealthy brother's desire that he should retire from business, the miller continued as follows:

What you are ready to do for me, I want you to do for Cristy. She is in danger, in more ways than one, and I am obliged to get her away from my house as if I was a smuggler, and my girl contraband goods. I am a bad hand at writing, so I leave Cristy to tell you the particulars. Will you receive her, brother Stephen? and take care of her? and do it as soon as possible?

Mr Stephen Toller's cordial reply mentioned that his vessel was ready to sail, and would pass the mouth of The Loke on her southward voyage. His brother caught at the idea thus suggested.

I have alluded to Giles Toller's sly look to his lodger, when I returned the manuscript of the confession. The old man's unscrupulous curiosity had already applied a second key to the cupboard in the lodger's room. There he had found the 'criminal stories' mentioned in the journal – including the story of abduction referred to by Lady Rachel. This gave him the very idea which his lodger had already relied on for carrying Cristel away by the river (under the influence, of course, of a soporific drug), while her father was keeping watch on the road. The secreting of the oars with this purpose in view, had failed as a measure of security. The miller's knowledge of the stream, and his daughter's ready courage, had suggested the idea of letting the boat drift, with Cristel hidden in it. Two of the yacht's crew, hidden among the trees, watched the progress of the boat until it rounded the promontory, and struck the shore. There, the yacht's boat was waiting. The rocket was fired to re-assure her father; and

Cristel was rowed to the mouth of the river, and safely received on board the yacht. Thus (with his good brother's help) the miller had made the River his Guilty accomplice in the abduction of his own child!

When I had read the correspondence, we spoke again of Cristel.

'To save time,' Mrs Stephen Toller said, 'I will write to my husband to-day, by a mounted messenger. He shall only tell Cristel that you have come back to England, and you shall arrange to meet her in our grounds when she returns. I am a childless woman, Mr Roylake – and I love her as I should have loved a daughter of my own. Where improvement (in external matters only) has seemed to be possible, it has been my delight to improve her. Your stepmother and Lady Rachel will acknowledge, even from their point of view, that there is a mistress who is worthy of her position at Trimley Deen.'

When Cristel returned the next day, she found that her uncle had deserted her, and suddenly discovered a man in the shrubbery. What that man said and did, and what the result of it was, may be inferred if I relate a remarkable event. Mrs Roylake has retired from the domestic superintendence of Trimley Deen.